Brief

from

E. F.

Mozart's Rabbi

Mozart's Rabbi

*The American Adventures of
Lorenzo Da Ponte*

A NOVEL

Ed Fiorelli

To order additional copies of this book, contact:
Xlibris Corporation
1-888-795-4274
www.Xlibris.com
Orders@Xlibris.com
106264

Once again, for Maria

AUTHOR'S NOTE

Mozart's Rabbi is a work of fiction, but a number of sources have guided the writer in the imaginative reconstruction of certain historical events.

Da Ponte's own *Memoirs*, translated by Elizabeth Abbott, Philadelphia, 1929, reprinted 2000, is a seminal source.

A concise, reliable account is Sheila Hodges, *Lorenzo Da Ponte: The Life and Times of Mozart's Librettist*, London, 1985.

For a scholarly study of Mozart's life and work see Robert W. Gutman, *Mozart: A Cultural Biography*, New York, 1999.

Edward Robb Ellis has examined and described the cause and effects of the cholera epidemic in a readable history, *the Epic of New York City*, New York, 1997. See especially, Chapter 18.

Opera in America, John Dizikes, New Haven, (Yale), 1993 presents an interesting "nuts and bolts" approach to opera as art, entertainment and business.

*   *   *

CONTENTS

LORENZO DA PONTE:
HIS LAST WILL AND TESTAMENT

I, Lorenzo Da Ponte, poet, scholar, collaborator with the great Wolfgang Mozart, his friend, his mentor and as great a genius as he . . .

I, Lorenzo Da Ponte, court poet to an emperor, gentleman grocer, notable impresario, teacher . . .

I, Lorenzo Da Ponte, prisoner of the Venetian state, bane of mediocre critics, and friend of the aspiring poet, champion of Italian literature, democrat and honest American, . . . now being of sound mind but unsound body, do hereby publish this, the last of my works, a final disposition of all my worldly goods, both real and immaterial. My friend and devoted patron Clement C. Moore, himself an author, inheritor of my most prized possession and executor of my poor estate, will doubtless condemn my use of the word "real", seeing it as the final confirmation of my blasphemy. He has often judged my hard-headed practicality and self-confidence as the mark of the charlatan. But I forgive him. He has been *born* American and thus takes for granted his charmed place in the world. His self-assurance is in the native blood, as indigenous as maize in the American soil. He has never felt the immigrant's need, his passion to succeed. But I, Lorenzo Da Ponte, native of Venice, have *become* American, for thirty years since have continuously tested myself, the cultivated poppy competing with the wild maize. Basta! Enough!

I forgive him. Besides, I can afford to be honest now, and declare that my self-confidence is on the rack. I know my death is near and like most men who have lived too long amid the delights of earth, I am skeptical of what lies beyond the grave.

As for the immaterial—those things that lie beyond the bequest of books or chairs or ormolu clocks—all the collected gatherings of eighty-odd years—I defer to the philosophers and theologians, men like Clement, and to posterity, to decide the value of that.

No regrets. I have done all I could have done with what was given me. I saw my opportunities, I took my chances. And here I am.

It could have been otherwise. But for a visit to my friend Jacques Casanova—he loved to be called *Cavaliere*—I might have stayed in Bohemia or Vienna or England and wound up like him, poor fellow, scribbling his memoirs in some dark cubby he called a library, taking time to stare at himself in his mirror while he sharpened his quill.

I remember paying a call on him a year or so before his death. He was librarian for Count Waldstein at the time and was put to work cataloguing a vast collection of books on necromancy most of which the count had never read and which he had relocated in a tower room facing the river. Waldstein had known of Casanova's interest in magic, and I suppose this post as librarian was as much a matter of superstition on the count's part as it was an act of charity for a fellow mason, eaten up by the pox and with what my friend Jacques himself called, the "Celtic humors".

He had been so hale a man in his youth, immune, it seemed, from any sickness or infirmity. I remember the healthy delight he took in watching the closing scenes of my *Don Giovanni* on opening night, clasping my hand afterwards and patting little Wolfgang on the shoulder, flattered that only his friends would know him enough, love him enough and be bold enough to present his life-story as an opera. I realize now that his vanity, so often misunderstood as bravado, was nothing more than an aspect of his good health.

But when I visited him in Dux that day, I feared he should see my shock at his appearance and come to realize his own end was near. I suspect he already knew. He was much smaller and thinner than I remember. His dark, smooth skin had taken on a ghastly yellow sheen. All his teeth were gone. The few stumps in his mouth were blackened and rotted, and he had a barbarous sore on his forehead that he kept aggravating with his quill, pricking it at odd intervals as we spoke.

As I entered the room I saw a frail, bespectacled Casanova sitting at a long table overflowing with papers and a scattered herd of leather-bound books. He was engaged in writing, and I could detect amid the silence of the room the gruff, hard sound of the nib as it scratched across the page, mingling with his own stern breathing, as if even the act of composition was an enforced labor.

He did not smile when he saw me, but rose stiffly, pushed his spectacles above his forehead and stretched out his hand. I took it, and gave it back to him, noting how he wiped it on his shirt afterwards, as if I were some loathsome carrion. Jacques had always prided himself on his knowledge of medicine. (Indeed, he had prided himself on many things.) He had a notion then that there were airborne sylphs, as he called them, a kind of alien *homunculi,* which somehow infected the blood through the skin. Perhaps he was mad at that time. The pox, after all, is notoriously ungrateful to its host.

Directing me to a chair next to the table of books, he took a seat across from me and scratched his bald scalp.

"It's good to see you after so long a time, my friend. I get so few visitors. What are you doing these days?"

I cleared my throat and told him of the few prospects for which I had high hopes.

"Prospects don't put food on the plate, Lorenzo. You of all people should know that. By the way, how's your little friend, Signor Mozart?"

"Dead," I said. "Four or five years ago."

"That's too bad. He did some good things."

"He was my protégé, you know," I said. "I was his great champion. I took him under my wing. My operas brought him the fame he so richly deserved."

"Yes," said Casanova. "I remember how you used to go about strutting like a cock in the hen house about your protégé, your jewel, your kindred spirit and all that."

I put my walking stick—the one Mozart had given me—on the table, expecting the cavaliere to admire it. But he didn't even look at it.

"What did he die of?" he asked. He tried to sound merely curious, but I picked up a note of alarm in his voice and said that I didn't know, but that Mozart himself thought he might have been poisoned.

"I'm not surprised," he said, looking at himself in the mirror opposite us. "He never took care of himself. A glass of nitrate water once a day for six weeks would have cleared away all those poisons. By the way, I want you to listen to something I've written."

I hoped my friend would not notice my squirming in the chair. Perhaps Jacques *was* the genius he had always claimed to be, but the shock of seeing him the way he was and the doubts I had about my own future at the time made me vaguely fearful of enduring one of his bouts of inspiration. He was particularly proud of his verse translation of Homer, but what *wasn't* he ever proud of? I was surprised when he got up, walked over to a side table beneath a gilt mirror and took from its case a violin. He began to play a little air. It was hopelessly atonal and dispensed within a few bars. I wondered what Mozart would have thought of it.

"Well?" he said.

Before I could respond, he continued.

"I know it needs some work, but it's not bad as it goes, don't you agree?"

"What about your writing?" I said. "I hear you're working on your memoirs."

"My memoirs are not for posterity, Lorenzo. They're for me. To keep from going mad. There are some fine things in them, I'll admit. For instance, I calculate I've slept with more than 120 women."

If he was waiting for my reaction he must have been disappointed. The truth was I didn't know what to say. But in the next moment he freed me from any obligation to say anything.

"That's not really true, you know," he said. "Women by and large are vicious beings. There have been only a few who loved me for myself. And I admired them immensely."

"But if you're writing to amuse yourself why exaggerate?"

"Who's exaggerating? Maybe there were 120 women. Maybe a thousand."

He rose and walked over to the side table, placed the violin gently in its case and began examining his face in the mirror. "How do I look, Lorenzo? Do I look all right?"

"Perhaps, *Cavaliere,* you need another dose of nitrate water," I said, failing to hide the mockery in my voice. Immediately I regretted my boorishness. To this very hour I deeply resent myself for such inelegant, misplaced wit.

"You'll outlive all of us, Jacques," I said in atonement. As it was, Casanova must not have heard me, for he returned to the table and sat down.

He began to write something, and then quickly crossed it out. He looked up, sighed, then threw down the quill and sat back in his chair.

"You mentioned prospects, Lorenzo. What kind of prospects?"

"A few things for Salieri. A book for a new opera."

"I don't remember Salieri as being very patient. None of those Austrian Italians are very patient, Salieri least of all."

"My protégé would have been able to do wonders with it," I said. "But the people today . . ."

"You're wasting your time, Lorenzo. Mozart is dead. The Emperor is dead. All the people who knew anything about art or music or love, they're all gone, except for you and me."

"Perhaps you're right," I said. "I haven't found a good patron, as you have, *Cavaliere.*"

I meant no sarcasm but this time Casanova seemed to mistake my remark.

"Ah, yes," he said. "Waldstein is a wonderful patron. "I have all this to myself"—gesturing by the sweep of his arm. "I've read every book in the Count's collection. There is a particularly fine edition of Hermes Trismegistus. Nowadays, especially, I have little to do but read."

"A rich reward for a life well-lived," I said foolishly.

"The Count is a great collector. Fortunately for me, he is *just* a collector. He enjoys looking at his books. Tool leather bindings fascinate him. I'm convinced that the very smell of them arouse his erotic ambitions. He reads only his account books. But in all this collection there is not one book on America."

"America is a young country," I said. "A sickly baby. It has done nothing to warrant a book."

"Speaking about prospects, Lorenzo, I have a suggestion for you. There's nothing here. You know that. But I've heard there are some rich pickings in America. The Count and his friend were talking one night a few weeks ago. I overheard them from the scullery where I was trying to entertain a young lady. She wasn't very young and I have my doubts about her being a lady, but let's not get into that. This friend was telling the Count about his adventures in New York, a wild, raucous place, he said, where everyone rushed to make money, cursed in many tongues and stepped over the pigs wallowing in the main street. Naturally, I was intrigued. My first thought was that there must be some beautiful women there."

"But none for you," I joked. "No countesses, no one of royal blood."

"Nor of peasant stock, I hear. Everyone is equal there, you know. It must be a dreadfully boring place for geniuses like us."

With much effort he reached across the table and slid one of the great books toward him. It was an ancient atlas, held together by leather strips; parts of it were already in deep decay. The energy required to move it caused him to breathe heavily and his next words were expelled in gasps.

"There is a map of America here," he said "I've looked at it many times."

He opened the book and together we sat staring at a page purporting to show a land mass of unfinished outline, surrounded by the words "terra incognita" and punctuated by puffing dragons and cartouches of dire omens. There were delineations of forests and mountains and scores of islands and shaded areas of vast blankness.

"This shows very little," I said. "How do we know it's America?"

"It's America, all right. But it doesn't tell anything. I have asked the Count to acquire a book about it. He says, 'of course', but I know he is only appeasing me. Besides, what does one know of any place from a map? Even Europe is 'terra incognita' if you haven't seen it for yourself."

"Still," I said. "There's probably nothing to see in America."

"Nevertheless, I would like to know something of the place. Those prospects you and I have been speaking of. It seems to me they would be growing on trees in America. I've thought many times about seeing this new world. Only five or six years ago there was nothing much keeping me from going. But now, there is the Count, and my duties here."

He closed the book, hefted it, and looked at the spine and then rose, carrying it as if it were an anvil to a smaller table beside a bookcase. He was proving to me that his duties were real, his devotion to them sincere.

"In any case," I said, "it's a dangerous trip."

Casanova laughed. "Ah," he said. "You haven't read my memoirs. I enjoy danger. There is a sensuous, almost erotic pleasure in putting oneself at hazard. I've risked danger at least 120 times!"

For a while we sat quietly, neither of us speaking, one of us trying to see what Casanova had been writing, the other gazing out the window.

"But you're right," Casanova said suddenly. "I'm too old to pluck the fruit from American trees."

He lapsed into silence again. Then he got up and began to walk towards the door to another room. "You should go, you know," he said.

"To America, you mean?"

"You've said it yourself, Lorenzo. You have no patron here. And with your protégé, as you call him, dead and buried, what's the use of answering the beck and call of a thousand mediocrities?"

I forget now what I said to him; perhaps something to the effect that I still had work to do. Whatever my response, it would not have mattered. By now my friend was moving off to the other room and would not have heard.

"Kiss a few of the beautiful American women for me," he said, closing the door behind him.

That was the last time I saw him. I remember that final meeting so clearly, especially now that I am in his place, waiting, as it were, for the end. But the difference between us is as wide an expanse as that 'terra incognita' on that ancient map in that ancient book. Unlike poor Jacques, I have refused to rust away under the pitiless countenance of an idle patron or an indifferent race. Although I did not know it at the time,

Jacques had taught me that inertia is death. There was no future in Europe for Casanova. Jacques was right about there being no future in Europe for me, as well. All I had to look forward to, as he had said, was answering the beck and call of a thousand impatient fools. That scene in the library was to teach me the need for courage, which was only another word for opportunity. If one door closes, you open another, even if it fronts a "terra incognita."

And so here I am, almost half a century later, having willed my possessions to a people of a new world, the map of which I have filled in with the dragons and cartouches of my own experience. I have made good here in my new country: raising my family, advancing my career, most of all securing my reputation and the respect of my fellow citizens. Mr. Moore will act diligently in fulfilling my bequests. I leave those things to him and rely on his good, honest judgment to render unto Caesar the things that are Caesar's. For me, it won't be long now before the last door opens and a "terra incognita" looms.

*   *   *

ONE

The Captain
How an Emperor helped
Lorenzo Da Ponte get to America

This one foreigner comes aboard. Navigating loose, you might say. Only a hard paper box cocked under one arm, the other hand clutching the damnedest cane I ever saw. Worth his passage by itself, I reckoned, though naturally I didn't let on at first. The head looked to be solid gold. He treated it with such landlubberly tenderness I knew right off this must have been his first time at sea, else he would have stowed it with his other valuables—not that he had much, only an old fiddle and a leaky crate of Eyetalian books—so that it wouldn't get ruinous salty when we run into rough water. Made me suspicious, like he wasn't quite respectable. Respectable passengers on my ship stow their goods below and never wear their fancy duds on deck once we leave sight of land and it commences to blow. But this foreign fellow was different. He wore this one outfit every day, clean but mended all over and kind of old.

But it wasn't just the stick or the clothes or his gear that made me take notice. And it wasn't his scared, uneasy look. The quick reason was that he wasn't on the passenger list. The agent had informed me of only nine passengers. There was a liquor merchant, a widow and her dead husband—he came in a box stowed in the hold—and half a dozen regular gents who make this crossing twice a year to take a sounding of their investments in New York. But there was no poet on the list. That's what he told me he was, a poet.

"Well, Mr. Italiano," I says. I forget his name now, but whenever he came on deck afterwards, I always called him Mr. Italiano because of the raggedy, female-like English he talked in. "Well, Mr. Italiano, how do you expect to find quarters aboard when I don't have you down on my manifest, hey?"

He bowed, looked me straight in the eye. Told me he hadn't time to bespeak his passage from the agent. Said he had decided quickly to go to America because there was no opportunity for good poets in Europe now, especially in England. Would take his chances in the new world, he says. I don't recollect if I believed him. He didn't look like the kind of fellow who took many chances, only the sure bets. I never knew nobody crossed the Atlantic on a whim unless he was a fool. And this fellow was no fool, though he must have thought I was, as you'll learn.

"You can't sail without the fare," I say. "I'm not running a fugitive ship. If you have spite against England you'll have to settle it ashore. If not, it'll cost you forty guineas."

He puts down his box and then glances about for a secure place for that stick of his. He leans it against the taffrail, then fetches about in the box and takes out a letter or some official-looking document. It had a fancy ribbon on it and was written pretty.

"Look here," he says, as if he's about to recite something. "This is a proclamation from your President."

And sure enough, he commences to read, like one of them actors in a play:

"To whom it may concern and greetings: The bearer of this is an honorable man, a poet and esteemed gentleman, inured to the comforts, delights and privileges rightfully bestowed on his person by gracious majesties in sundry European courts. I shall consider myself deeply obliged if you show him all the courtesy and respect due a man of his extraordinary parts. Yours, Sir Thomas Jefferson, President of America."

He looked confidently at me, as if expecting I would fall at his feet and beg him to take my cabin. But I came upwind of him and hit him broadside:

"And what am I supposed to think of that, hey?" I say. "Thom Jefferson can heave full sail across his own seas, but *I'm* the President of *this* ship!'

"But this is your own President!" yammers Mr. Italiano, waving the document, making sure I could see the seal and ribbon.

"Even the President needs forty guineas to take passage, my friend."

I reckon that if President Jefferson himself ever did board the *Columbia* I would carry him for free, just for the honor of the thing, you understand. But this Italiano fellow riled me, so confident was he that I could be so easily gulled. He had better learn that documents of this sort—"oblige me and bow, etc."—may work in Europe, but they don't amount to a skiff's ballast over here. I expect Mr. Italiano will find that out soon enough. I got a notion he done up the letter himself and meant to fob it off on some poor fool in America.

Mr. Italiano shook his head and muttered something in his native lingo. Then he fetches up another letter with more pretty writing. "This is from the Emperor," he says.

"What emperor?" I say.

"Joseph," he says, like I had done him some grievous wrong. "His Majesty, Sovereign Ruler of Austria and the Holy Roman Empire."

"Ah, yes," I says. *"That* emperor! Forty guineas, if you please!"

Still another letter bobs up, from some duke or other, commending Mr. Italiano to my good will.

"Forty guineas," I say.

Italiano was working up a sweat now, and I'll admit I was beginning to enjoy it.

"I suppose you've tried all this on Mr.Priestly." (He was the agent.) "It didn't work on him, either."

"Captain," said Italiano. "I regret that men of such high repute like me command so little respect from men like you. I must get to America. I haven't got forty guineas, but I will not grovel."

"What *have* you got?" I say. I had already decided to put him off, but was having fun watching him squirm. I hate these foreigners who lack humbleness and think they're better than us, especially fellows like this who want to pay with bows and fine words instead of with good hard cash. Just then my eyes went to the taffrail where Mr. Italiano had reposed his walking stick. The fellow must have seen me looking at it because he spoke right out: "I cannot part with that."

"That's hardly worth forty guineas," I say, shrewdly.

He stood quiet, fixing his eyes on the rigging.

"Well," I say. "What's it to be? Either you've got forty guineas worth of goods or it's England for you."

"I've got some fine books," he says, looking at the beat-up crate at his feet. "But I should hate to part with them."

I laugh. "Don't worry about separating yourself from them books", I say. "Can't use them, don't want them. What else you got?"

Italiano snorts in disgust, shakes his head, reaches inside his coat. Fetching a faded green purse, he counts out six coins.

"I can spare only these," he says. An ill assortment of Austrian, French and English pieces, they was. I suspect he was trying to confuse me with their different values. I sensed that he had more real money about him and told him so.

"What little I have is for America," he says. "I need to live, to start a business if need be. These you may have."

"That's white of you, Mr. Italiano. Give them to Sir Thomas when you see him. What else you got?"

Into that paper box again, scrabbles around, brings out a handkerchief folded over. It looks like pure lace, all fancy work round the edges. I remember seeing one like that on some English milord who made a crossing some years back. Brought six traveling cases aboard, all stowed in his cabin, so I don't know where he could have slept. But that was his pleasure, I'd say, since he paid his fare and didn't try to unload some flotsam on me like this Mr. Italiano here.

He begins to unfold the handkerchief and holds up a medal, not real gold, but with a nice red and green ribbon.

"This is from the Emperor himself," he says. "A testimonial to my poetic gifts."

I take a good gander at it but it don't look like it's worth no forty guineas so I give it back. "I guess it's England for you, my man," I say.

"Listen," he says. "I won't be humiliated. I am a true poet. Unused to this kind of haggling, I see now that you have your own code. If I'm to thrive in my new life I'll have to learn it."

"There's no `code', as you call it," I say. "Pay as you go. It's forty guineas and no haggling."

I had just about had my fill of Mr. Italiano and was about to ask the mate to put him off when he plunges into his box again and fetches up a red case. At first I think he's trying to bribe me with a box of fine segars, seeing him caressing the case, like it was a pet.

"This is my final treasure," he says. "My only tangible claim that the world once acknowledged me as a great poet."

"It had better be worth forty guineas," I say.

"O Tempora! O Mores," he says, shaking his head.

He holds the case like he was about to present me with a choice segar, like I said. But it turns out that when he raises the lid all I see is half a dozen tiny spoons staring back at me.

"The Emperor Joseph, may he rest in peace, personally presented me with these," he says.

I guess he must have seen my sour expression because he quickly adds, "Solid silver."

Now I didn't want to appear too anxious to jump at his offer. I wasn't so sure at this point that the spoons were worth the price of passage. They were too small to be of any use, unless you were only three feet tall and had a head the size of an apple. On the other hand, they may have a certain draw for Mr. Peale's collection of curiosities. In the next instant I calculated that the spoons would bring at least forty or fifty guineas in England, maybe more in America.

"Well," I say. "How do I know they're real silver?"

"Do you doubt a personal gift from the Emperor would be anything less?"

"I never knew the Emperor," I say. "And how can I be sure that the Emperor himself knew they were silver?"

Oh, Captain Grunge, I say to myself, you are a sly one, you are! No landlubber could steal upwind of you!

Just then Mr. Italiano slams down the lid and makes to go.

"You are a *caffone,*" he says.

"Tell you what," I say—I knew I had him—"I'll give you passage in exchange for these spoons, but you're a few guineas short. Throw in that walking stick and I'll settle the difference with the owners."

I see Mr. Italiano widen his eyes and turn down his mouth.

"I cannot do that," he says. "This was given to me by a man whose genius was very nearly equal to my own. His gratitude and affection for me sprang from motives of respect that you could not possibly appreciate."

"Take it or leave it," I say.

"I will leave it," he says. "There must be at least one ship for America with no pirates at the helm."

"No use getting mad," I say. "Business is business. Tell you what. I'll give you passage for them spoons. You can keep your stick, but if you want victuals it'll cost you extra."

Here Mr. Italiano just about gives up. I watch as he reaches into his coat pocket and pulls out his purse, He opens it, grabs my hand and empties the purse into it. Then he shakes the purse once or twice to show me his money's all gone.

"You've ruined me," he says.

"Here", I say, giving him an Austrian coin. "I'm not a mercinous fellow. Welcome aboard!"

*   *   *

TWO

The Widow

How Da Ponte came to write his first "American" poem

At first I thought he was a lord. His clothes were clean but old and threadbare, not the sort of outfit for a prince, but he could have been a lesser nobleman, maybe a count or duke. He spoke in a pretty accent, like a Spanish *grandee,* maybe, or an Italian *cavaliere,* bored with life on his villa in the Umbrian hills and now en route to New York on the last leg of his grand tour of the known world. He might even have been traveling *incognito,* as I've heard some royalty often do. At the very least he was a gentleman, in spite of his appearance, not like the other men aboard who pretended to be strolling on deck—cluttered with rope and other things of the sailor's trade—pretending to converse with each other about business. The only business they were engaged in was covertly peering at me over lowered eyebrows as I took the air. They thought I didn't notice their glances, which made me uncomfortable, a poor widow bringing her husband back home, having to endure everything in their looks but real sympathy.

My own sympathy now was with this gentleman. He was leaning over the rail, rising to his toes, his face ashen as he retched into the sea. I knew exactly how he must have felt. I was seasick myself once, and the only fellow to offer any help was the man who eventually became my husband. And now here was this gentleman, heaving at the rail, more concerned about how he must have looked than how he felt.

"You'll pardon me, I'm sure," he blurted out, trying to keep in control.

"Don't concern yourself," I said, patting his back, as one would an infant's. "It's best to let it out. You'll feel better."

He seemed embarrassed and shrugged away my hand. Then, as if taking my advice, he retched again and spewed out his breakfast, some of which blew back into his face. That's when we both knew we were on the wrong side of the ship. As I helped him across the deck he was so mindful about his lost dignity that his pale, sweaty face actually took on a burnished glow.

"This is the worst experience of my life," he said weakly.

The breeze and fresh air, more gentle on this side, did him some good, but when he dropped his fine walking stick—he had been holding it under his arm—and became excited at the prospect of its rolling overboard, I quickly picked it up and, giving it to him, sat him down on a roll of canvas.

"This is a big ocean," he said. "The poets had no idea. I hope I did not embarrass you."

"Don't be silly," I told him.

"A fine woman like yourself, in proper mourning, as I judge from your widow's weeds, doesn't need any further burdens."

"A widow is still quite capable of helping others in need, sir, and I can certainly take care of myself if need be. The Lord has regard for his sheep."

He began wiping his face with his handkerchief and we sat for a few moments, not saying anything. Then the gentleman, sensing the awkwardness of the situation, offered me his condolences on the death of my husband.

"Luddy was such a good man," I said. And with that, I pulled out my own handkerchief and dabbed my eyes. "I'll miss him very much. He was a man of great courage."

I waited for the gentleman to respond, expecting a courtly inquiry about the nature of my husband's bravery. He might have remarked about my own need to be brave. Instead, he sat quietly. I glanced up from my handkerchief and observed him staring resentfully at the swells that rolled beyond the rail and I couldn't decide whether he was truly compassionate over my loss or still smarting at his own loss of dignity by the impertinent sea.

"He was very brave," I continued. "Brave and dedicated."

My gentleman still remained quiet, although now he seemed to have gotten over the sea's insult and was engaged in deep thought.

"Sometimes I think his devotion to duty was greater than his love for me," I said.

Then I sighed. This brought him round. "That is the great theme of life," he said. "Poets from time immemorial have been inspired by that most noble of conflicts—the struggle in the human breast between love and duty."

I continued to dab at my eyes.

"Oh, I know he loved me—in his own way. But you're right. There was always that ambition, that urge to accomplish the great goal of his life. Pitiless, I call it. A pitiless desire that excluded even me from its ultimate attainment".

The gentleman merely fondled his walking stick and nodded.

I sniffled. "Did I mention that Luddy was a missionary?"

"Indeed!" responded my gentleman. "That *is* a calling that demands great dedication. In that sense we are kin, your husband and I."

"You've heard, then, of the Ludlow Smoot Church of the Royal Wounded Conscience?"

"Regretfully no," the man with the fine walking stick said. "My stay in England was brief, very brief."

"Luddy's church—our church—began in America," I said. "His vocation came to him one day on Broadway as clear and as certain as the grace of the Lord."

"You misunderstand me, madam. I meant that, like your husband, I, too, am dedicated to a noble profession. In my younger days I gave some thought to taking holy orders, but the call of the muses was too strong. You see before you, dear lady, not a clergyman, but a humble poet. As to the Church of the Conscience, I'm coming to America for the first time, and am not familiar with it."

"The Ludlow Smoot Church of the Royal Wounded Conscience," I corrected. "You're not alone in your ignorance of the church. Most Americans aren't familiar with it, either. That's the problem. And now, now, with Luddy below—May he rest in peace—no one will ever know of it."

I wept into my handkerchief and my gentleman began to comfort me—with utmost decorum, of course. He took my hand and patted it encouragingly and I began to tell him of Luddy's thwarted vocation, how day after day, saddened by the Americans' dearth of spiritual values, he ceaselessly preached to them in their banks, their taverns, their temples of commerce. How his preaching fell by the wayside as unto him the Americans hardened their hearts and closed their purses. How he went off alone to pray for guidance as his body grew lean and his strength decayed. How at length the Lord smote Ludlow Smoot, throwing him into a mighty stupor when an immense pig tumbled him into the muddy street we Americans call Broadway. How he awoke a changed man, his vision clarified, and his life's work affirmed. He was to preach not to the Americans. He was to leave his native land, to voyage into the Old World, there to preach unto the heathens of England."

"Heathens? In England, Mrs. Smoot?" questioned my gentleman.

"Heathens of the spirit," I said, looking at him closely. "Those dukes, earls, viscounts and all the other members of the king's council of the privy. All the godless whose wealth and power blind and ensnare them."

My gentleman smiled. "Most royalty I've known—I've worked for many of them—are the most tight-fisted lot on earth. They were least generous with poets."

"Luddy worked tirelessly among them," I said. "At first it was a dispiriting task. Viscount X was always amused but hardly devout. The Earl of Y shook his hand, but never invited him to dinner. The Marquis of Z bowed courteously but always kept his hands in his pocket."

"Exactly!" said my man.

"Then one day his labors bore fruit—or so he thought. Duke Somebody offered to back Luddy in building his church. With the Duke's support it was an easy task to hire the workmen, on credit, and to renovate the ground floor of a building he owned on the Strand. People said the building once served as the apartments of the duke's favorite female companion, now dead. But Luddy was a tolerant, forgiving man. Let him who is without sin cast the first stone. Was not Mary Magdelene among the chosen of the Lord? Judge not and thou shalt not be judged. Even the Father Himself judges no one, see John, chapter 5, verse 22. And so arose the Ludlow Smoot Church of the Royal Wounded Conscience, attended every Sunday by earls and dukes, and viscounts and barons and marquees."

I had been doing well to this point, but the thought of Luddy and of what happened next brought me to tears again, and the gentleman of the fine walking stick soothed me by patting my hand, urging me to buck up. So I continued:

"But Satan stirred. Luddy could hear him in the heavy breathing of those viscounts and dukes nodding off in the best pews, could see him behind the closed eyes of the lords and earls slumbering in theirs. Then Satan struck, just as he had afflicted Job, the Lord's other favorite."

"Ludlow died."

"Not then, no," I said. "But came the day when Duke Somebody walked into the sacristy after services. Luddy had just given a wonderful sermon on how the Lord loveth a cheerful giver. Duke Somebody put his hand on Luddy's shoulder and smiled. He told him how much he had admired Luddy's sermon; how pertinent it was to his—the Duke's—present situation. And I saw Luddy's heart break. Luddy knew what was coming. The Duke went on to explain that he had befriended a poor, homeless young woman; how it was unseemly for her to stay under the same roof as the Duke; how the Duke had determined to set her up in her own establishment. And that was the end of Luddy's church. The Lord was evicted, his place filled by Satan and the Whore of Babylon."

"But surely there were other benefactors," the gentleman remarked.

"I've said already that the English were heathens. There were no other benefactors. Only hard hearts and closed fists. Luddy's spirit was broken. He was never the same again. For many days he wandered aimlessly about the streets, desperate, damned, and disillusioned. One night, while laying his head on my lap—we had taken a room in a boarding house in the East End—Luddy sighed and closed his eyes forever. His last words to me were 'Take me home.' And now I am respecting his wishes."

This last remark was too much for me, and I cried inconsolably. My gentleman had the good sense to let me alone, and when I could cry no more he rose from where we were sitting and extended me his arm. He seemed suddenly energized, as if my misery were a source of his own renewal.

"Would you allow a poor poet to do something for you?"

"I couldn't take your money," I said, dabbing my eyes again.

"I would not insult you by offering money. I can give you only the benefit of my muse."

I was now convinced that my gentleman was really a prince, traveling, as I suspected, *incognito.* If I had learned anything in England it was that the truly rich never wish to appear to be so. The real aristocrats never flaunt their wealth; never make it a center of public display. This gentleman was obviously quite rich. I had only to play my cards right and I would soon learn of his personal generosity.

"I would like to honor your late husband."

"Yes . . . ?" I twisted a corner of the handkerchief around my finger.

"I would like to celebrate his life . . . ."

"Yes . . . ?"

"In verse."

"Oh!"

"A life of dedication such as his should not go unheralded. Take me to him."

For the first time I began to grow uneasy.

"Dear sir," I said. "My husband is dead!"

"Of course, of course. Please do not misunderstand me. I wish to write a poem on your husband, but to do so I want to surround myself with the proper associations. Creation involves the right perspective. I once worked with a man, a genius, who didn't need such associations. He could write in a barrel. When we worked together I could write in a barrel too. We seemed to feed off each other. He's been dead these last twenty years. I'm on my own now and have had to climb out of the barrel and do what I can, the best way I can. I need the associations, the spur to my muse."

I had no idea what he was talking about and I have a notion that he didn't know, either. Some rich men of quality are so peculiar that way, only their money keeping them from the lunatic asylum.

"It isn't a very nice place, the hold," I told him, hoping to dissuade him. "It's leaky and damp."

"Tis not as damp as the river Styx," he muttered. Then he looked at me, as if he had gotten an idea. "Before we go down you must do something for me."

"What is that?" I must have sounded suspicious, and who wouldn't, after all?

"My muse must be paid."

He probably saw the quizzical, even resentful look on my face because he quickly resumed, as if defending himself.

"But only a token, I assure you. Those associations I told you about. Give the muse but a shilling, offer her a guinea, and she will respond. I will write your husband a *memento mori* worthy of his glorious life."

"A guinea," I said. "That much?"

"A shilling then. You may throw it into the sea, if you wish. As I said, it is but a customary token. Here, give it to me and I shall redeem the muse."

Reluctant, but wanting to humor my prince, I gave him a guinea, but instead of throwing it overboard he put it in his pocket. Then he quickly took hold of my arm and together we made our way below.

The hold was dark, lit only by our lanterns and a few random slats of sunlight that seeped in from somewhere above us. We walked carefully, like drunkards, hunching our backs and ducking our heads as we went along the wooden rib cage of the ship. I could hear the ocean just inches beyond the bulkhead and could feel small puddles slapping at my shoes. Luddy's coffin was wedged against one rib so that the space narrowed as we approached and my gentleman nearly hit his head.

We put our lanterns on the lid, and I placed my hand on the coffin and patted it affectionately. My gentleman stared at the simple pine box and for a moment I was frightened by the thought that he would want to have a look at Luddy. The rich generally feel privileged to act in such odd ways that I had a sudden vision of this prince prying off the lid and gazing fervently into my husband's face. I was saved from such a fear, however, when my gentleman merely bowed his head. "God bless him; may he rest in peace," he said. "Now to my poem."

From his pocket my man produced a piece of paper. Moving both lanterns close, he rested the paper on the coffin, pondered a moment, and then began to write. Once or twice he paused, bit his lip, stared at a lantern and then continued. Several times while he worked I began to say something—it was so lonely there in the hold—but he brushed his arm in the air and said, "Shhhh," so I waited for him to finish. In a few minutes he was done, and I could see him moving his lips as he read over the piece.

I was expecting him to present me with the poem, perhaps in a flourish, maybe with a bow, his walking stick tucked under his arm—he never let it out of his sight—for if nothing else his efforts had cost me a guinea. Instead, he picked up a lantern and with his other hand brought the paper up to the light and began to read it aloud. First, he apologized for not yet having a title. That will come later, with the polishing, he said. Next he cleared his throat. Finally, standing erect, he commenced:

> "0 weep for Ludlow Smoot, for he is dead,
> With ne'er a rough-hewn tombstone for his head.
> Who brought his zeal across vast Ocean's breadth
> But found, instead, the cold, calm clutch of death.
> Forsaking all the New World's petty scorn
> He sailed for England, there to be re-born.
> His reputation shines without a taint:
> He left New York a man, returns a saint.
> So sing for Ludlow Smoot a low lament

Who slipped his life with days but barely spent.
And let us mourn a seemly season past,
Our griefs then stow and into Time's maw cast.
His Truth will thus survive the bell's last toll,
Forever thrive in mankind's mind and soul.
Then Ludlow Smoot no longer will be dead
But in his lover's heart wait just ahead."

He finished, and then looked at me, as if expecting a response. For a few moments I said nothing and we stood there beside Luddy's coffin, the light from the lanterns keeping his face in shadow. I thought I detected a smile on it and I was embarrassed and a little afraid. What was I to say? That it was a very good poem? That he read it beautifully? These rich aristocrats are so quick to take umbrage; I didn't want to offend him and lose my chance. But somehow, perhaps because of Luddy in the coffin next to us, I felt the urge to send him away.

"I'm feeling rather faint," I said.

"Forgive me. This is, indeed, a dreary place. Let's go back up." He took my arm. "Thank you, sir," I said. "I'd like to spend some time alone with my husband. I'm sure you understand."

"Of course. I shall go back to my room and re-copy your husband's tribute in a fine hand, adding a title. Then I shall present it to you, on deck, of course, when next I see you."

"You're very kind," I said.

The prince took a lantern and I watched with growing calm as he made his way up the hatch.

When his light disappeared I took my own lantern from the coffin lid and whispered the name of my husband. He answered me with two quick knocks from inside. "All clear, Luddy," I said.

The coffin lid slid open and Luddy sat up, quickly climbed out.

"It's about time," he said. "Couldn't you get him to write the damn thing on deck or in his cabin?"

"I couldn't help it, Luddy. He wanted to get inspired or something. I was worried that you wouldn't be able to climb into the box fast enough."

"I heard everything and saw you coming," he said. "It's hard enough to live down here during the day, but it's hell in that box, even if it is only for a few minutes at a time."

"I know, Luddy, and I'm sorry. But we agreed, you know that."

"Yesterday one of the crew came down to look for something. I was lucky to get back in just in time."

"A few more days we'll be in New York."

"Thank God," Luddy said. "I can't take much more of this. I'm growing a hump."

I began rubbing his back and thought, oddly, of my prince.

"We agreed, didn't we, that this was the best way to get to America?" I said. "Since we didn't have the fare for both of us. Besides, Captain Grunge gave me a rebate on you. He likes pretty widows."

"What about this other fellow?" Luddy asked.

"I think he's a prince or a duke," I said. "He's very well-mannered, very well-spoken."

"But does he have any money? That's the important thing."

"He's a prince who features himself a poet," I said. "He's eccentric enough to charge me a guinea for what he calls his muse."

"You mean we gave *him* money?"

"I told you, Luddy, he's eccentric. A prince like him, I'm sure he's rich." Luddy smiled. "Well," he said. "I reckon you're right. You're a genius in this sort of thing, my dear."

"Don't worry," I said. "We've baited the hook and the prince is a big fish. Meantime, it's getting dark. Come up to my cabin later. I'll have some food for you. And remember, come daylight you've got to get back into the hold. Let me worry about my prince. I'm sure he's worth a fortune."

* * *

THREE

The Patron

*How and where Lorenzo Da Ponte
introduced himself*

I first met the man in Riley's on the Broadway road, directly
after a scuffle with Van Briesen's pig. He's a good fellow—Van
Briesen, I mean—but where his pig is concerned he's usually
irascible, ill tempered and unreasonable. More than once I've
warned him to keep the animal off the main thoroughfare, to
pen him in the common ground set aside for swine, especially the
bad ones like Dutch, but Van Briesen just laughs and dismisses
me with a wave of his hand.

"He's got a mind of his own," Van Briesen protests. "Just like
some people. Besides, Broadway is a public street and I'm the
public."

"Yes," I tell him. "But you treat it like private property, as if
it's your own pigpen."

"Dutch is a good boy," Van Briesen says. "He don't mean no
harm. And besides, he eats better on Broadway. He's doing you
a favor, cleaning up the fruit rinds and cabbages."

That was largely true, of course, and on any other day I might
have been more forgiving of both Van Briesen's attitude and
Dutch's greedy predations amid the garbage of Bowling Green.

But I had no patience this particular morning when the nasty creature came rooting past me, spattering mud on my new boots. I had just received them the day before from the merchant ship, recently arrived, together with an order of fine English cravats and a dressing gown of exquisite Italian silk. Goods from Europe were scarce enough these days, without having them ruined by my neighbor's indifference, as good a man as he may be in other respects. So I was not in the best of humor as I made my way to the bookshop.

Just outside I saw an old peddler's wagon lashed to a half-dead nag who greeted my approach by arching its tail and spewing its business onto the ground with an insolent thud. The canvas top was rent with holes, as if the thing had circumnavigated the globe in a hurricane. Hanging from the side was a sign that read: "L. de Ponty's Wagon: Everything You Need." I wondered what, indeed, could fill the vast mine of mankind's desires that could possibly be contained within the bowels of this conveyance? He was a magnificent peddler, to be sure, who could redeem such a promise! I subdued a strong temptation to peep inside the wagon and entered the shop.

Riley himself was not behind the counter; I heard him rummaging through his stock in the back room. Behind me I also heard a quiet rustle, as if someone were turning the page of a book. I turned and saw a tall, fragile-looking, stoop-shouldered man, about sixty, standing by a table near the window squinting over a volume of verse. He looked up suddenly and smiled politely, then returned to his reading. He was dressed in clean, well-tailored clothes, once elegant but now twenty years out of date. By his side leaned an attractive walking stick, richly worked with a gold headpiece. It struck me that despite his age and his fragility he didn't really need the stick.

A full minute must have gone, only the sounds of Riley's search and the stranger's turning of a page between us. I don't know why I should have begun to feel awkward. There was no reason I should have felt obliged to speak to this man, nor he to me But I got the sense that now and then he was secretly glancing up at me from his book, taking a sounding, as if lying in wait.

Just then—and thankfully—Riley came out, carrying several books.

"Here you are, signor," he said. "I can let you have them at a discount. I'm glad to be rid of them. Not much call for these Eyetalians."

The signor smiled, his chin jutting from his face, floridly pock-marked. His demeanor took on the cautiously assertive posture of the inveterate negotiator.

"That is a lamentable fact," said the signor. "Americans know little of the glories of Italian literature. They read only English books."—here he looked at me—"They wear English clothes. One day I shall convince you all of the singular beauties of the Italian language and literature."

Here he began examining the bindings, hefting the books as if calculating their value by weight and gently stroking the covers.

"What is your price?" he asked, not looking up.

Riley thought for a moment, seemed to scan the fellow as if he himself were a rare book and then mentioned a figure.

"Yes," said the signor. "And they are worth it, to be sure."

Now it was the signor's turn to ponder. Riley stood with one hand on his hip, the other on the counter, a stain of a smile on his face.

The signor raised a finger, as if to call for silence or attention and turned to leave. But before he was out the door Riley stopped him.

"Wait a minute, signor. If you're going out to the wagon, I'll spare you the trip. I can't take any more trade. I've already got two old hats and one of them doesn't fit. Thank you kindly, but it's got to be hard cash."

The old man seemed disappointed, but sensing that he had an audience he turned back into the shop, cradling his walking stick and smiled. When he got to the counter he put down his stick carefully and then drew out a worn, green velvet purse, carefully counting out the coins, studying them first to be certain of their denominations. Riley looked away, trying to put this foreign gentleman at ease. Then he saw me standing near the counter and came to his own rescue.

"Good day, Mr. Moore," he said. "What do you need?"

"As a matter of fact," I said. "I'm interested in one of your 'Eyetalians.'"

I had, indeed, some interest in one of his Italian books, though not to buy. I had lent my copy of Dante to a friend and now had need of a quotation from the 'Inferno' for a sermon I was preparing. Riley had been as good a reference librarian as he was a bookseller and when I told him that I merely wanted to verify a quotation I was sure he would let me peruse a copy.

The signor had finished counting out his money and when he heard me mention Dante his face refulgent. His dark eyes came alive.

"You are conversant with the great writers of Italy?" As he spoke he grabbed his walking stick and veritably jumped to my side. I was startled by his enthusiasm which nourished such agility. He brought his face close to mine, as if he were about to confide a great secret. As he spoke his mouth literally collapsed about his lips. He had no teeth, and in his surge the words aggressively tumbled out.

I told him that I admired Dante as one of the world's great poets.

"Dante is famous because he is Dante. He is like Shakespeare. We read him and call him great, even if we do not understand him. But what of the others? Do you know the others, Ariosto and Tasso and Alfieri, all the great writers of Italy? My dear sir, their works would well fill this very room." Here he waved his arm in proper dramatic emphasis.

"This is Signor Da Ponte," Riley offered, as if to spare me from an admission that there were parts of Shakespeare and Dante that I didn't understand. I suppose I must have looked shocked, or least puzzled, for this fellow had blown to bits my conception of peddlers. I admit I didn't know what to think about him except, perhaps, that he was a grand imposter, a kind of latter-day Haroun el-Rashid, travelling up and down Broadway, supplying the world's wants within the shallow cup of a covered wagon.

"Lorenzo Da Ponte," the signor said, expecting me to recognize the name. He bowed stiffly. "And with whom do I have the honor of conversing?"

Riley did not offer here, though I would have been saved from bowing and introducing myself if he had. My friend Riley considered himself a staunch democrat, believing that a calculated indifference to the awkward fumbling of his friends was proof that he respected their democratic rights to make fools of themselves. And so at this moment he chose to mind his own business, and allowed me to pursue mine.

"Mr. Clement Moore at your service," I said at last.

Sensing my awkwardness, Da Ponte held out his hand and smiled.

"Are you a literary man yourself, sir?" he said.

His question surprised me. By implying my literary ability he was neatly insinuating his own, intimating that he himself was one of those "others" in Italian literature.

"My works have been seen in all the major houses in Europe," he said. "Even in England, though I know that we Americans are not on good terms with the English these days. I mention it only as a fact, since I have no interest in politics. Are you at all familiar with my work?" His eyes kindled. "Italian books are not popular here yet, but one day they shall be, and soon."

I was quick to note his claim to be an American and grew vaguely suspicious. But there was, for all his implicit self-promotion, a natural honesty, a candid avowal, as if to say, "This is what I am, take it or leave it." And if at first I was caught off guard, I wanted also, for some reason, to believe in him.

"You must know *Figaro*. What of my opera *Figaro*?"

At this point my own eyes must have ignited in recognition—not with the fame of Da Ponte, but with his reference to a scandalous play I had heard of during my student days at Columbia.

"My opera, *Figaro,* was the sensation of the world twenty years ago. A man named Wolfgang Mozart wrote the music. Wonderful music it was, but my poetry made it live. For months, during that entire season, everyone talked about nothing but *Figaro*. I discovered Mozart, you know. He had already done a great deal of music. But his first venture into the field of literature—that, sir, was my doing. My poetry gave his music wings."

Here he presented his walking stick. "Look here," he said. Holding it before me he turned it round so that I could gaze appreciatively at the gold headpiece. Da Ponte told me that it bore the insignia of the Order of Masons.

"A gift," he said. "From my friend, Mozart. From one genius to another. Observe, if you will, the workmanship."

Looking closely, I could see an engraving of what looked like a bridge.

"This is a reference to my patronymic, 'Da Ponte'. Wolfgang and his little jokes. He could be generous, but also dangerously extravagant. This is worth a fortune. I wouldn't part with it for any sum, not even for a whole library of great Italian books."

Da Ponte picked up his books and once again appraised the bindings. For a moment I was struck with the thought that the fellow was about to offer me an opportunity to buy his stick.

Meanwhile, he must have observed me craning my neck in an effort to read the titles of his books. He brought them almost teasingly to his breast.

"One of your own works?" I asked.

"Ah, no. I am afraid the world has not yet caught up with me. I fear that perhaps it has even passed me by."

Putting one of his books into my hand, "The great Tasso," he said. "His numbers are exquisite."

I told him that I was familiar with Tasso's epic of the Crusades, but only in translation. My Italian, I admitted, was not yet vigorous. At this he smiled, almost wistfully and began to recite, from memory, what must have been the very work. I was astonished by the man's power; his recital impressed me with its sonority and clarity of phrase. Even Riley, who was not a man easily imposed upon, stood with his arms folded, smiling in admiration.

By now Da Ponte perceived he had an audience and began gesturing dramatically. Then he changed the tempo of the verse, reciting quickly, his eyes ablaze.

> "Non piu andrai, farfallone amoroso,
> Notte e giorno d'intorno girando,
> Delle belle turbando il reposo,
> Narcisetto, Ardoncino d'armor."

"Bravo," Riley shouted. "Bravo, Tasso."

Da Ponte bowed to his audience. "The first part was Tasso, surely," he said. "But the last was Da Ponte."

Riley laughed. "Then Bravo, Da Ponte, too!"

Now Da Ponte, the peddler-poet, surprised me once again. Turning to me, he bowed and held out the book.

"My dear Mr. Moore," he said. "Allow me to give you the Tasso. As a memento of our new acquaintance."

If I had begun by suspecting him of being a charlatan, I was now ready to accept him as the real thing, but this last act of generosity disturbed my equilibrium. Call me a snob, if you wish. Lorenzo Da Ponte was not, after all, the bogeyman. But I admit that among my faults is a tendency to be suspicious when I ought to be trusting. A healthy skepticism in a man of the world may not be a virtue but in a man of God it comes as close to a vice as treachery itself. I could not help looking askance at this fellow. For all of Da Ponte's courtliness, he looked somehow tender, vulnerable, as if upon a fragile touch, a mere glance of skepticism, the figure of the gentleman would fall back and in its stead would emerge the form of the scoundrel.

In spite of this, I regained my balance and mutely accepted his gift. I should have thanked him, but the expression would have sounded oddly lame. Da Ponte didn't seem to notice. Perhaps he was letting me off the hook, secretly enjoying a triumph, allowing me the distillation of his finest generosity.

Whatever it was, he smiled benignantly. Tucking the other book under his arm he shook my hand, bowed, and bid me good day. I watched as he climbed into the wagon and scuttled up Broadway in a jangle of dust. He almost ran over the squealing Dutch, darting out from under the wheels, in pursuit of the vagabond cabbage.

*　　*　　*

FOUR

The Bookseller

How Lorenzo Da Ponte was taken for a democrat; and how Clement Moore attacked Mr. Thomas Jefferson

As soon as he came into the shop I saw through his shabby clothes to something more genuine. Friends had advised me that he was a sharper, or at least that he thought of himself as one. Frankly, from the looks of his clothes and the hungry way he smelled out a bargain on the books I sold him, it seemed to me that others had gotten the better of him more often than not. Certainly he didn't look like an Abbé, either. Word has it that he was a priest back in Europe, but that surely was a long time ago, and what a man *was* in Europe doesn't count, only what he *is* here. One thing was certain: there was more pie than piety in him. I knew from the minute he spoke that beneath his faded lace and street-worn brocade he was a true democrat, right down to the very buckles of his shoes. He had an Eyetalian accent, but handled English very well, carefully, like a man counting out unfamiliar money. I had seen him pass by the shop from time to time, sometimes on foot, but more often in that wagon of his which, like his clothes, had seen better days. Always when he passed he would glance into the window, and I frequently imagined that in that glance he took in every detail, as if it was going to be of use to him later on. Once or twice he came in to buy some books, but never paid in cash, only goods. At first I didn't mind; it was worth talking to him and I could see that he was the genuine article, although I couldn't say why, exactly.

On the day when he met Mr. Moore he had come directly to the counter, not even browsing about the shelves. He asked me straight off if I had a book on the art of distilling. What kind of distilling, I asked him. He looked at me right in the eye—another way I had of identifying him as a democrat—and smiled. He told me that he had met some people in England who were making a pretty fair living distilling spirits. He had determined, he said, that since he couldn't make a go of it by "molding his own words", he could at least get on by "helping other men mangle theirs."

He seemed to think that this was funny, and then suddenly his face glowed. He was reminded, he said, of his days in Vienna, twenty years ago. He and a fellow named Mozart and a singer named Kelly made the rounds one night of the taverns and grog shops. It was after the success of his *Figaro.* They drank all night and sang all night, but the astonishing thing was, he went on, that this Mozart never got drunk enough to slur even one note, though the three could hardly walk by the time the watch made his final rounds at dawn. Now a count or a milord, or an Abbé, for that matter, would never admit even to an occasional carouse, but this fellow, as I've said, he was a real democrat. He hung on his own hook, taking a man for what he was, and not for what he wore. He liked a spot every now and then and wasn't ashamed to admit that he put on his own britches every morning instead of having his "man" or his slave do the job.

I told him that I had nothing on the making of whiskey, but I did have an account on the history of the whiskey rebellion that occurred out west about ten years ago. To this he merely

shook his head. Then he put his cane—it was really a fine piece
of work—on the counter and rubbed his chin. He said his name
was Lorenzo Da Ponte, the famous court poet, and that he had
arrived in New York to start a new life. This clinched it for me—I
mean about his being a democrat. But I said to him that he
would have a hard time being a court poet in New York because
the courts here only fined you, jailed you or hanged you, and
there was nothing poetic about that. Da Ponte nodded. Yes, he
said. He quite understood the injustices of that sort of court.
The ones he was familiar with in Europe had their own ways of
exacting justice, punishing not so much a man's body as his soul.
His reputation, he declared, had been drawn and quartered as if
he had been caught robbing the emperor's larder. That man was
pretty handy with words, for a democrat.

I reckon I knew what he meant, but he left no doubt when he
took his stick from the counter, put it behind his hip and leaned
on it, staring off as if the wall were an open window. Then he
told me how he had gotten a slew of enemies because he was a
genius and they were only well-groomed, well-bespoken drays
that dumbly pulled the dung cart of literature. I guess I smiled
at that, seeing his own wagon out front, ready to be carted off as
kindling if he let it stand without keeping his eye on it. He said
that the Viennese were a suspicious, envious bunch and that the
Eyetalians had become better politicians because of it. That was
his problem, he said. He wasn't a politician, but a genius. Only
he and that fellow Mozart were authentic, honest.

Anyway, I guess Da Ponte suddenly realized the confidence
he had been letting me into, because just then he flailed his stick
in the air as if throttling the subject for good.

Then he asked me if I had stocked any books of Eyetalian
poetry. Now the only customer who has ever asked me for
books like that was Mr. Clement Moore, the clergyman. He is
a real gentleman, too, and as sensibly devout, I suppose, as any
Protestant has a right to be. Some of us think he's too smug

and a bit stand-offish. But I've known Mr. Moore for years—he must be pretty near thirty now—and I can tell you that when all is said and done he is at bottom a fine man, a kind-hearted man who just happens to be afflicted with a case of caution fever.

Sometimes, I'll admit, the power of his opinions seems to work him up. A few years ago he wrote a pamphlet called "Observations on Mr. Jefferson's *Notes on Virginia* which Subverts Religion and Establishes a False Philosophy". I remember the title because Mr. Moore had it printed at his own expense and sent me 500 copies, 460 of which are still in the back room. Of course I don't regularly read all the books I sell, nor would I want to. But with Mr. Moore's book I felt especially obliged at least to see what all the fuss was about. I have to be honest, I made it nearly to page four before my mouth went dry and my eyes burned with a strong will to close. Some people, like Mr. Moore, are interesting and honest in their own persons, but when they get hold of a pen and put it to paper they suddenly become living, breathing lexicons, sounding more like a fancy bill of lading than men of flesh and blood. For the first few months afterwards he used to come in every other day, asking about his "Observations", but in a while he let sleeping dogs lie and that was the end of it. Gentlemen don't write books for money. And they don't write them for prestige. Certainly the Moore's have plenty of both. If you ask me, Clement Moore harbors some secret literary ambition, and one of these days he is likely to produce something that won't remain for very long in somebody's stockroom.

It was this same Mr. Moore who just happened to have come into the shop as I was in the back, searching for those Goldoni and Tasso volumes that I couldn't get rid of and that were gathering dust atop a hogshead near the pile of Mr. Moore's "Observations".

I heard the tinkle of the bell and looking over the counter from the stockroom I saw Mr. Moore walk in with that slow, deliberate gait of his, as if he were made of glass. As he entered I could imagine Da Ponte surveying the younger man. I didn't hear either speak.

When I came out with the books Da Ponte leaned over the counter in expectation. I told him that I could give him a discount, but as he examined the books he tried to pay in goods, but I told him that I couldn't manage that anymore; he'd have to pay in cash.

Here I saw Mr. Moore scanning Da Ponte, checking him out like a reference from a book. As a matter of fact Moore had come in to inquire about a reference in Dante's *Inferno,* from the eighth circle, I think, of the flatterers and con men. Da Ponte knew the reference. I could tell from the liveliness of his expression and by his difficulty with staying quiet. After a bit of palaver I introduced the two. Da Ponte nearly jumped onto Moore, like a starving man suddenly presented with meat. He gave out that he was a poet. Mr. Moore seemed impressed. He was even more taken, I judge, with Da Ponte's cane.

The court poet sensed that, too, giving Mr. Moore a good look at the thing while he himself delivered a discourse on how valuable it was. He said his friend Mozart had given it to him in testimony of his genius, not using those words exactly, but I knew what he meant, and I knew what Mr. Moore must have been thinking: he wanted to like Da Ponte, to trust him. But that well-founded caution of his kept him at a safe distance.

Then Da Ponte said he was devoted to Eyetalian poetry. He especially liked Tasso, he said, and then commenced to recite from memory a portion of his poem. Da Ponte was great, very impressive. He wasn't cheating, you see. No flailing about or waving his arms. I don't know Eyetalian, but I know when I'm being tricked and there wasn't any trickery here. He simply *knew*, he simply *understood*.

When he was done he turned and gave Mr. Moore Tasso's book. Then he bowed and left. I can still see the expression on

Moore's face. It was as if he couldn't decide whether to be thankful or suspicious. His predicament reminded me of that old prophet in the story of the Trojan horse. That horse was at the gates, but this old fellow railed mightily against its being brought in. But the gods didn't like his attitude. They sent a monstrous snake. It got him and his sons and that ended the discussion. Now Moore was like that old prophet, except he wasn't quite so sure of the danger. Though he might want to rail against the horse, he still kept one hand on the bridle.

But that last gesture on Da Ponte's part that was the clincher. It confirmed what I knew from the first: cane and all, that man was a true democrat.

*   *   *

FIVE

The Tenor
How Da Ponte acquired his walking stick and how he and Mozart ate macaroni

Michael Kelly to Antonio Salieri   25 March, 1811

My dear Salieri:

New York is, indeed, a fair-sized city, much larger than I had been led to believe from acquaintances returning with lurid reports about wild men and assorted cud-chewing entrepreneurs. But it is not so large that a brisk walk wouldn't take you to its boundaries, beyond which farms and country houses suggest a modest prosperity.

I was just descending from the coach that had dropped me on a muddy, tree-lined street they call Broadway when whom should I see but our old chum, the poet Lorenzo D. What I saw when I descended was only his back as he climbed into a ramshackle vehicle that looked like a peddler's cart. Of course, it would not have surprised me, knowing his persistently precarious fortunes, to see him riding in a tumbrel in these latter times, but even then I wasn't sure it was he. The figure I glimpsed was rather crabbed and somewhat shabby, but the walking stick was clearly his; one couldn't mistake it, for all the pride he took in it. In any event, it is a pity that he did not hear my hailing as he rattled off.

The last time he and I spoke, you'll remember, was in London. He had hastily fled Vienna back in '88, narrowly escaping the jaws of debtor's prison. In spite of your letters of recommendation and support, he had managed to arrive in London as poor as a church mouse, with only the clothes on his back and that infernal walking stick by his side. He had gotten into more debt—Mr. D. wasn't the sort of man who could long stay out of it—and was about to present me with an opportunity to advance both mine and his own fortunes. Mr. D. was always embroiled in some such scheme or other that would make the plots of his own librettos read like a schoolboy's primer. This time he was involved in some intrigue with a rogue named Rufus Taylor who was attempting to head up a theatrical company to rival Drury Lane. This Taylor fellow is a real jackanapes who will assuredly run the company into ruin. He is even more susceptible to disastrous schemes and swindles than Da Ponte. I've been told that Taylor hates the Italians. If that be true, I have no doubt that his alliance with Mr. D on that occasion must surely have been short-lived and quite exploded. I know for a fact that Taylor has been involved in a number of duels. He is an altogether odious creature.

Of course, I never did trust any of that sort, as I had long ago learned to rely only on the certainty of my own genius—and, naturally, on what your own good will and supreme influence could purchase toward my success. But I digress. Lorenzo, as I've said, had approached me with that absurd swagger of his, brandishing his beloved walking stick and promising me a sultan's argosy for an advance of ten pounds on his next venture. Naturally, I declined. It was at this point that he put his hand on my shoulder and leaned confidentially into my face.

"So certain am I of this enterprise," he said. "That I am willing to put up my prized possession as surety."

Here he laid his stick in my hand. It *was* a beauty, I must say. But you well know I have achieved a well-deserved place in the world by eschewing the blandishments of devils and angels alike, and I could make no exceptions on this occasion. I told him I could not allow him to risk losing his own soul, so passionately devout as he was about that stick. It was a sentiment, I daresay, that Mr. D could not fail but to admire: flamboyant yet subtle, it was as apt a *bon mot* as any turn of phrase has a right to be.

Did I ever tell you, by the way, how our Mr. D acquired that stick?

I was with him when Mozart gave it to him, though it was for a reason far different from Mr. D's own account of the story to his legion of admirers, that is to say, creditors. We had been celebrating the opening of *Figaro*. Each of us had, indeed, our own share in that wonder! Lorenzo naturally appropriated most of the credit to himself—he was always running on about *his* opera, *his* poetry, *and his* characterization. Never mind that my own conspicuous role as the first Don Basilio was acclaimed even by the Emperor himself! You'll remember how I had convinced Mozart that Don Basilio ought to be played with a kind of lisping stammer, much in the manner of Da Ponte himself, and when it was time for my entrance I grabbed a cane and strutted and cavorted like Da Ponte. Leaning on my cane, strutting like a peacock, for a full ten minutes, I lisped, I stuttered. The audience was moved to gales of laughter. Even Mr. D laughed at the joke when he saw how effective I was in the portrayal. Naturally, I took my bows and was forced to interrupt my impersonation by acknowledging the gentlemen in their boxes and the young ladies in their rhapsodies, flinging their billet-doux at my feet. Some of their propositions, by the way, were quite brazen. I could very well have enjoyed their favors at my own convenience, but I would have none of it, not then, at any rate. You know my personal convictions about the harm that can be done to the vocal chords by the untimely practice of venery. An artist must commit himself to a life of practiced deprivation, at least while in the service of his lady Muse!

In this connection, I must thank you for your praises of my performance. Even though you and the Emperor thought lightly of the music—too many notes—and less of the scandalous subject matter, as an artist I nevertheless must set myself apart from personal opinion and obey Euterpe when she beckons. I shall have no truck with mediocrity.

But to continue: We were celebrating *Figaro*, as I've said. Mozart was aglow, like gunpowder ready to fire. Since none of us had eaten since morning, he suggested that the three of us "escape", as he put it, to a tavern. Lorenzo quickly recommended a place operated by one of his countrymen, nothing more than an unseemly hut somewhere near a moneylender's establishment with which, doubtless, Lorenzo must have been well-acquainted. A bizarre little jakes of a place, it squatted off the side of the road, an unreadable sign hanging from the brow of the roof. Inside, the main eating area was dark, redolent of garlic, a few habitués, drunk as lords, sitting by the hearth.

Mozart seemed perfectly comfortable in such a place. I have known him to be insufferably fastidious about his music—becoming churlish if someone even coughed while he was playing the pianoforte—but in matters of everyday life he was rather elegantly indifferent. Frequenting such establishments was as natural for him as attending a fancy-dress ball. He gave not a fig, either for footmen in golden livery or butchers in bloody smocks. It was all one, with him. Like Da Ponte, I'm sorry to say, he was a man of republican tastes and too easy adaptability. Such men could hardly expect to gain the approbation of princes, as have you and I.

At any rate, this particular place, said Mr. D, was famous for its macaroni, then becoming popular in Vienna. Each of us ordered a bowl, and when the stuff arrived, looking for the entire world like some vermiculous heap, I was reluctant to engage. Suddenly Mr. D performed a feat that I could scarcely credit even now. Thrusting his fingers into the bowl, he scooped out a mass, twisted it about his fingers and brought the whole thing to his mouth. Mozart laughed. "Bravo!" he exclaimed, and proceeded to do equal service. As it proved, Mozart was better at the game, owing to his long, agile fingers.

No sooner was the first bowl emptied than Lorenzo called for a second. "Come, O'Chelli," he said. "Join us." (Mr. D, you'll recall, could never appreciate that an Irishman could have a surname that did not begin with an "O". To him I was never "Kelly", but always "Ochelli".)

That night, as I watched, Lorenzo and Mozart dueled over their bowls of macaroni, each inventing a new flourish, a novel improvisation of the wrist, their heads tilted, mouths widened to receive the stash. Even the drunkards by the hearth were sufficiently moved by the performance, sitting erect, tilting their heads in imitation, opening their mouths and widening their eyes as if witnessing some fabulous thing. After four bowls, Mozart surrendered. He was such a little man, so spare of frame. I marveled he was able to consume as much as he did. But there was no doubt as to the winner of that match. Da Ponte devoured one more bowl and for good measure drank another bottle of wine.

A few days later the victorious Mr. D. received a gift from his eating companion—a remarkable walking stick. It bore the inscription: "In admiration for his genius. From W.A.M."

That duel was the only contest I recall Mozart's ever having lost. Certainly it was the only one to which he so graciously acceded defeat. I remember a particular dinner party at our friend Storace's house at which Mozart displayed an equally good-natured but more tenacious competitive energy. Lorenzo was there, of course. It was Mr. D who suggested that his "protégé", as he called him, his "protégé," Signor Mozart, could out-play any other musician in the house. Lorenzo himself went round taking up a subscription, as if he were selling tickets, God help us, while poor Mozart quietly took up only his viola. I suspect that the little man really needed no abetting. He would as soon play in a brothel as a drawing room. As for Lorenzo, his role as impresario was as welcome as sugar to the coffee. That night Mozart played gallantly, fiercely, those long, slender fingers that had done so noble a service to macaroni now serving up a crystal confection to a hushed audience. Lorenzo pocketed some seven pounds—a true genius, indeed!

But now to my purpose. You know the reason I left England for this backwater. Mr. William Dunlap, playwright and impresario—a factotum of no mean ability I'm told—has asked me to supervise a possible production of my *Blue Beard*. I can hardly refuse, especially since he has offered to pay all expenses. I shall, of course, sing the principal part, that goes without saying. I was to meet him at the ship but he sent word that he was indisposed and would set me up at the American Hotel until I was refreshed enough to meet with him the next day. This hotel is a dreary place, like some of those dreadful holes we were lodged in back in Naples in the early days. There are even some loafers sitting like savage island kings on what they call here "the stoop". All in all it is a most uninspiring place, squatting as it does amid the unpruned elms and beeches along the Broadway Road which itself terminates at a stand of blackberry bushes marking the border of some Dutchman's 'fife'. Across the street is a bookshop, equally as dreary, but I suppose this is the best the Americans can offer and *noblesse oblige*.

While my bags were being transported to this esteemed lodging house I decided to take some refreshment and found myself in a place called Tontine's not too far from the hotel. It was pleasant enough and a rather imposing structure with a broad verandah and a luxurious aroma of coffee coming from within. I understand it is a popular rendezvous for the transaction of business and other commercial enterprises, and I did see some tradesmen there and some carters unloading their cargoes of barrels unceremoniously against the side of the building. I supposed then—and I but think all the more certainly now—that I must have wandered into one of those bastions of democracy we've all been hearing about. Everything about the place seemed "democratic" in the worst sense. Though the spirits were good, and the codfish excellent, the place had about it a sense of subdued frenzy. People seemed to be buying and selling everything, even the aroma of the coffee, yet nothing tangible changed hands. Bustle was everywhere, but it was oddly an aura of bustle rather than a manifestation of physical activity. In short, business was the order of the day. Engagement was all. Whatever social or artistic interest these Americans showed, nobody talked about it at Tontine's.

I have been invited to speak at a gathering of *literati*, by the way. Only but shortly arrived and already a sought-after guest! Doubtless the group will be made up of an odd assortment of pretentious poets and would-be scribblers who fancy themselves heirs apparent to the Muses solely by virtue of their being Americans. You'll remember, I'm sure, that repulsive Yankee who appeared in our midst a number of years ago, like Elijah in a fiery chariot. He arrived with an intellectual handbag of small arms and a belief in his ability to blow up the literary cannons of *Blackwood's*. For a while he was the demi-god of London, gaining the public's attention much in the manner of the king's fool or a two-headed goat. He preached on the irrelevance, as he put it, of the past, scolding our poets for their reliance on tradition and our historians on their enslavement to genealogies. "I sing a new song," he would howl. "The sun rises in the west." Naturally, he soon grew tiresome: the same ship that carried him hither bore him back to New York, his own cracked ambition stowed, like broken chinaware, in its hold. So much for the fools who talk about literature but never produce any of it. The only person who did not outright laugh at him was poor Da Ponte, and we both know how the old signor has literally fallen off the edge of the earth. If that fellow in the wagon on Broadway was our Mr. D, I have no doubt that despite his flipped fortunes he will find a way to come up heads.

I make an end of this by advising you that I have effected some changes in some major scenes of *Blue Beard*. Where the princess, now disguised as a serving wench to the Barbary pirate (who is himself the disguised Sultan), accidentally drops a handkerchief belonging to the prince-regent, I have inserted an aria of some sixteen bars in which she sings plaintively of her life as a scullery maid. The effect of irony is thus enhanced, don't you see. I think the touch is fetching, and quite brilliant. In Act Two, scene twelve, I bring on Sir Hugh shackled and enchained. His aria, "O feckless me, poor shackled one," will very likely induce a tear, as it did in London. You know the present public mania for chain scenes.

In the finale, where Sir Hugh is about to be shot dead by the pirate queen, I have invented a cunning piece of work: Sir Hugh sings an aria, "No Dastard, nay, nor Bastard, I" in which he refuses to repent his past wickedness, even though he knows he shall be doomed to perdition. The aria is a full sixteen bars and is in 3/4 time, in the manner of the new-style waltz. I know the piece will be smashing, especially to Americans who are agog at the least suggestion of violence. There are times, my dear Salieri, when I am frightened at the thought of my own genius.

Your obedient servant,
Michael Kelly

*   *   *

SIX

The Composer
How Da Ponte received his first commissions and from whom he received them

Antonio Salieri to Michael Kelly   27 April, 1811

My dear Kelly:

You are exactly right in deciding to go to America in an attempt to advance your fortunes, and especially to promote your opera *Blue Beard*. There, you may be sure, a man of your talents can freshen a career already growing stale among the overweening judgments of the fickle public here. I have heard that America has, from the beginning, become a popular destination for those wishing to build upon the shambles of their own lives forged here in Europe. I have no doubt that many of these are thieves and scoundrels, but that among the others, like you, there are genuine possibilities of a fruitful intercourse.

One of the chief regrets of my life—too numerous to advert to here—was in ignoring the opportunities that the New World may have afforded. I must say that I never really agreed with our friend Buffon. He always declared the Americans to be a degenerate race and the land a stony, savage wilderness inhabited by Indians and brutish adventurers who would sooner break your head with a tommy-hawk than listen to an aria. I am of the opinion that America will one day make a noise in the world and that sooner or later we must all look westward. But I have never been able to turn my opinion into action in this regard. Greatness called to greatness and it was my duty to hearken to its call. My duties here in Vienna as supreme opera director for his Majesty had kept me fully engaged for many years. Now that our Emperor is dead, and the world turned upside down, it seems that Fortune's wheel has turned away from me, and plans for my "American sojourn", alas, come too late. In any case, I am glad, as I said, that you are earnestly committing yourself to the venture.

Of course I remember both DaPonte and Wolfgang Mozart. The former always struck me as *too* persistent, *too* aggressive, while the latter never deigned to be aggressive enough but lived in the cocoon of his own conceit. It was Mozart's assessment of his talent that put me, as well as others, at a distance. He flourished for too long in—how shall I say it—an unshakable sense of superiority. The irony is, my dear Kelly, that sometimes I fear he was right, as every day now I hear more of the dead man's music and less of my own. But I am convinced that Fortune has her ways. She will smile on both us as brightly with her next turning.

As for Da Ponte, I remember his doing several librettos for me—his first, I believe. They were, admittedly, workmanlike and dramatically effective. *Rich for a Day* and especially *Auxur: King of Ormus* played well enough, but there were certain notions of his that I could not countenance. In some ways he was a butcher. His insistence on brevity, for instance, often resulted in his foreshortening certain scenes, forcing me to cut whole passages of exquisite music, glissandos, prestos and fortissimos that were veritable food for the gods and would certainly have proven a feast for his majesty! I think that was why I never called upon him for more work; there were plenty of others—like Righini, for instance—who could give me what I wanted with fewer headaches.

I remember Da Ponte as a lean, hawk-faced man with a sheaf of letters recommending him to me and a healthy, well-fed attitude to carry them in. He was dressed in serviceable clothes—neat, clean and inexpensive. They looked new and his discomfiture obvious. Aside from this, he seemed to carry himself with just the right mix of confidence and deference. Not servile, by any means—I would have dismissed him immediately on that account—he seemed to understand his true position and the nature of my own power to help or hinder him. I was extremely busy, making final arrangements for my revival of *The School of Jealousy*—a personal favorite among my vast *oeuvre*—and I remember my annoyance at being besieged most of the morning by the importunities of lackeys, the counsels of minor clerics and the pathetic effusions of would-be poets. And then there was Da Ponte, standing there in his twill frock coat and his sheaf of letters.

"On what grounds should I speak to the Emperor on your behalf?" I asked him.

Da Ponte smiled, as if privy to some mutual arrangement. "Perhaps simply on the grounds of my being a fellow countryman."

"My dear Signor," I said, anxious to disabuse him of his notion about blood being thicker than water. "The man who bakes my bread is a fellow countryman. The man who cooks my fish is a fellow countryman. The man who powders my wig, he is even a relative. I do not need another baker or cook. Nor certainly another relative."

"I beg your pardon, Maestro. I meant that as a fellow countryman I can offer my services as a poet."

"I knew quite well what you meant, Signor Da Ponte. But I do not need another poet, either, nor does his Majesty."

Da Ponte bowed. "I beg your pardon once again, Maestro, but let me affirm that I will bring honor to you and the emperor. I am wise enough to know my limitations and skillful enough to work quickly and to specification. And most assuredly I will not be satisfied with inferior work."

Here he began taking some letters out of the sheaf and offering them to me.

Deliberately I withheld. "That's very good of you, I'm sure. But are you implying that I or any of the Emperor's people . . ."

"I say simply that I have the ability, the integrity, the resolve to serve you well."

During this conversation, as I've said, Da Ponte did not behave like a man seeking favor. He looked me directly in the face always, and never once looked away or fidgeted with his hands or papers or with anything a lesser man would use to save himself from self-perceived groveling. Take Righini, for instance. You'll remember him, I'm sure. You would have thought I was the archbishop of Milan, for all his kissing my hands and his incessant bowing, as if he had swallowed a rainbow. It's enough to turn the head of an ordinary man. An ordinary man would easily see himself as perfection's vicar. But I have grown immune to such flattery. Like Caesar, I am unmoved by the pleas of the rabble. But this Da Ponte fellow was as direct and confident as any talented man without a position could be.

"I will consider your petition," I said, beckoning my man to take his letters and then to show him out. I had already made up my mind to speak well of him to the Emperor. At the very least, he impressed me as a man whose very earnestness alone might very well carry the burden of any insufficiency of talent. But it would not have been politic to embrace him at this first interview. Besides, I had the duty of teaching Signor Da Ponte the lesson of patience and humility and to exercise fully the prerogatives which I myself had attained over so long a life of dedicated service. I liked him and had heard good things of him, but to take him on immediately would have been tantamount to admitting between us an implicit equality. You and I both know the rules in this regard, my dear Kelly.

As to Mozart, what can I add? I know that he was a friend of yours and can appreciate the extent of your admiration for him as a musician and composer. I myself, of course, am not unmindful of his present-day reputation, nor can I ignore the noise that his fame produced back in the '70's when he and I were just commencing our careers, though to be sure he was just a boy at that time. Even then, I'll admit, I was impressed. But I tempered my enthusiasm when I recalled the number of prodigies whose flame burned brightly for a while, in time only to become *extinguished* rather than *distinguished*.

These events would have taken place, incidentally, within a year or so of my first elevation to greatness: I was only twenty-eight when my *Europa Recognized* became the first opera commissioned for the opening of La Scala in Milan. And after that success, I startled the world with my immortal *Cave of Trofonius*!

But returning to Mozart. He was, as everyone knows, a vulgar little man, whose vulgarity was often tolerated, even excused, in the interest of his obvious musical ability.

He was as natural a composer as I had ever known. His judgment and taste were exquisite, though too fine to a fault. The texture of his music was often too thick, too complex for the human ear, his Majesty's most especially. His greatest flaw, as I've tried to make clear, was his pride. An instance should make clear what I mean.

I saw him once at a party hosted by Caffarelli, a wild man on the stage, as everybody knows, but remarkably congenial, even kind, off it. I had just been accepting the compliments of Madame Veneer over the success of my *Trofonius*. You know the work. It has been hailed as the greatest opera buffa of the age and it's a pity you did not have a chance to sing the title role. I have always admired the timber of your voice and have always declared your "portamento" to be the finest I've ever heard. At any rate, Signor Mozart was there; the little gnome was clutching his glass of punch as if it were a beloved pet—I understand that he was inordinately fond of the stuff. There I was with Madame Veneer, whose appreciation was revealing itself in tender touches at my sleeve, and there was Signor Mozart, across the room, gripping his punch and looking toward me with a wry smile. I was expecting a nod, at least, but the man drank down his punch and without any sign of acknowledgment—I don't say *obeisance,* mind you!—he turned his back on me and moved off to see Caffarellli's new billiard room.

Believe me, sir; I am not exaggerating his impudence. I could excuse him if he were simply a rude fellow. But even my cook, even my baker, has better notions of his place than did this upstart composer without any prospects. Mozart's biggest flaw, as I've said, was his pride. He suffered from a species of spiteful independence which rendered him incapable of showing proper deference on just those occasions when proper deference was demanded. In short, had his knowledge of promoting his musical abilities matched the abilities themselves he would have been a wonder. Who knows, he might have even eclipsed you, my dear friend!

As for that absurd talk of my having anything to do with Mozart's death, you have better sense than to trust those vile rumor-mongers whose capacity for malicious gossip is their own only talent. Mozart was a voluptuary. You have only to behold "Figaro" to observe how its defiance of taste and decency has turned with poetic justice against the life of its perpetrator and composer. Mozart's own life-style should have brought on his death sooner than it did. We've both known for years about his carryings-on with the likes of upstart sopranos, and the precipitant illness of his last year should not have been surprising, judging by his tavern bill and his work habits. And while we on the subject, I have always suspected that Da Ponte himself was a bad influence on Mozart. But that is matter for another day.

I note with interest your emendations to the original *Blue Beard*. Of course I am but a humble composer and teacher; librettos are not my forte, although as my former student, Herr Beethoven has remarked, my advice is more often sound and correct, if not inspired. Allow me, then, to comment with all good will on your remarks:

First, the scene in which the princess sings, "sotto voce" of her career as a kitchen wench is all wrong. Sixteen bars for such an aria is too short. Sixty-four bars, suffused throughout with the lamenting strains of an English horn, would be just the thing in evoking such a plaintive mood. Your orchestration for this aria calls for five flutes. Flutes? My friend, they are too shrill to achieve the effect of "happy melancholy tinged with irony" that you are trying for. You will afflict the American audience, already inured to war whoops, with a bad case of goat bleat. No, English horns are what you want.

In this connection I was disappointed that you chose not to use Caffarelli at the premier. He has an amazing voice; its clarity is remarkable and his "vibrato" the best of any singer in his class. It is true, of course, that like the rest of his kind, he is pompous, even rude. But castrati like him do not grow on trees, my dear fellow, and if one can ignore his outbursts—like the time he presented his buttocks and passed wind onto the first violinist for being a trifle too forte with his *pizzicatti*—one would judge him to be worth every *fart*hing. Ha ha!

Second, Sir Hugh's song as he faces certain death and the hideous prospect of eternal damnation is oddly reminiscent, I'm afraid, of a scene from your great friend's work. I refer, of course, to Mozart. Do you remember a little thing of his that opened in Prague about twenty years ago? I believe our mutual friend Da Ponte had a hand in that fiasco, as well. As for your own genius, be not afraid; it will do you no harm.

Now as to tempo. The waltz, my dear friend? The waltz? What can you be thinking of? Surely the use of such a vulgar rhythm betokens a decadence more appropriate for a bordello—one of Da Ponte's perhaps—than an opera house!

Even a ghastly "siciliano" would be less contemptible in such a context. Of course, from an aesthetic point of view, the decadent waltz *would* reflect Sir Hugh's own evil ways, but certainly a successful artist such as yourself ought to able to suggest decadence without indulging in it.

By the way, in Act Two you may want Sir Hugh to fight a lion *while he is singing* his aria "My heart is sere, by Love's hot tear", instead of simply having his man declaim in ruthless recitative that lions have been known to inhabit those woods. Trust me, the audience will devour that scene sooner than your lion will Sir Hugh!

Do please consider these changes. In any case, you will understand, I hope, that my comments are not meant in the least to be invidious. I am confident that you will take no offence where none is intended.

In the meantime, I look forward anxiously to news of your American triumph, and am, sir,

Salieri.

P.S.

By the way, I've recently learned that Rufus Taylor has been in America now for a year or more. I know that you dislike him. I myself have never been counted as one of his friends, although he has always tried to do his best, albeit begrudgingly, in mounting my own operas in London. I can well believe the accounts of his laxity and incompetence, but these are not as disturbing to me as those charges suggesting his jealousy and spitefulness to the Italians. I have no direct knowledge of his being as big a blackguard as people say. I do remember poor Da Ponte having a run in with him on several occasions, but he has never done any wrong to *me*, I can tell you, and so what other people think of him is no affair of mine. Let the little fish eat the other little fish.

If you see him in your travels about New York do mention me to him. Perhaps there is yet an opportunity for an American performance of my work.

S.

*   *   *

SEVEN

The Historian

How Lorenzo Da Ponte conversed with Mozart during a game of billiards

For my projected *History of the American Theatre* I am including a section on non-American playwrights as a kind of cautionary tale. An illustration from the lives of such men will serve as a reminder to those of us who may forget the shameful situation endured by most playwrights nowadays, who have no patronage and no pension. Like commercial drummers who must hawk their wares at the nearest corner, playwrights today must barker their works to an indifferent trade, customers less interested in drama than in the price of a ton of ten-penny nails. A case in point is the situation related to me by a recent acquaintance, Mr. Lorenzo Da Ponte, late of London and Vienna.

I met him in Tontine's, where he was sitting at a rear table with a member of one of the most esteemed families in New York. The two were chatting animatedly. In front of Da Ponte a pile of dishes was spilling over with oyster shells and the remains of a chunk of codfish. The other man's spot by the table was as lean as Jack Sprat's plate. Da Ponte was an ancient, crooked fellow, with a large nose and rather shabby clothes and whose face looked imploded. I recognized his name as soon as we were introduced, and as I shook hands and sat down at the table I suddenly realized that this man represented a generation and a society for which I had nothing but scorn. He stood for the bad Old World of courts, corruption and privilege, of preferment by political intrigue rather than merit. What I did not know at the time—and what I was soon to find out—was that Da Ponte too, for all his claims of success, had begun as a peddler of poetic wares. Like the very commercial drummers we American playwrights have become, he had learned early how to make friends and how to produce honest, high-quality goods.

After the table was cleared I asked him politely if he had given any thought to writing a new play, but he declared that the stage was no longer attractive to him, that he had become a kind of anachronism. "I am an American now. My talent, my genius, was for Europe, which was the whole world then. But it matters little here and now. I leave drama to younger men who are not afraid."

When I suggested that perhaps he was right, that carving a literary career in America was not for the faint of heart, Da Ponte smiled.

"Dear Mr. Dunlap," he began. "That can be said about all aspects of living. One must work hard to live hard. Besides, I didn't mean that I was afraid of writing drama again. I will vouch for my reputation on the basis of *Figaro* and the other things I've done. No, I've finished with drama; it is now time for something else."

"You mean, then, that you'll be substituting one form of huckstering for another?"

"That's rather unfair of you, Dunlap," said Da Ponte's companion, he of the lean table. "Signor Da Ponte cannot live on air. I think we Americans ought to be more enlightened about artists than we are."

I agreed, of course, with our friend. A commodity they may be, I admitted, but a rare one, and worthy of wise nurturing.

"We shall see," said Da Ponte, smiling. "I am not afraid of opportunity. I yearn for it."

Here he beckoned for the waiter and ordered a round of spirits. "Please permit me," he said and fetched up a few coins from a faded purse that he carefully creased and put back inside his coat.

"You were talking about nurturing the artist," Da Ponte said. "That would imply your recognizing him first and then having the means to sustain him. Years ago I was the first to recognize my protégé. But I was merely his equal and had no power to convince the world of his greatness. Politics and ignorant men did the rest. I speak, of course, of Mozart."

He laid his walking stick on the table. The gold head and brilliantly worked inscriptions caught my eye. Doubtless it had the effect on me that Da Ponte had wanted. He smiled, placed his hands on the stick, sat back and continued:

"I had been invited to a party at the house of an illustrious gentleman and had been making the customary obeisance, doling out the expected compliments. The room was filled with my countrymen, headed by the influential Salieri to whom I had attached myself—things were done that way—and by whose means I had recently been appointed court opera poet.

"Before long I took a stroll about the grounds, still uncomfortable amid so many notable and powerful men. My clothes were new, but I had sunk my entire fortune on them so that I was in effect the most well-dressed pauper in the house. In those days I was living on expectations, though my stomach was a realist; it would not thrive for long on promises and flattery. From somewhere off the garden veranda I heard a laugh and a sharp clattering sound, as of bones rattling in a cave. Curious, I followed the sound and found myself at the entrance of a large paneled room illuminated by a crystal chandelier that blazed with the light of a hundred candles. It was the only source of light in the room, as round the walls only shadows loomed, and the smoke from the pipes of equally shadowed men. In

the center was a billiard table, several men in shirtsleeves standing about it. Straddling the table, one knee propped on the green velvet surface, a little man in gold breeches was bending over, presenting me his rump as he balanced himself for a shot. He had removed not only his coat but his wig as well, and his mop of fine blond hair hung in disarray about his head. He had also taken off a shoe; it lay on its side by the table leg. I could see a small hole in the toe of his hose.

Turning his head, he saw me at the door. "Am I called for?" he said.

At the same time, the little man sighted his cue and took his shot. It must have been an errant one, for he suddenly threw down his cue and let fly a stream of passionate profanity, violent invectives on body parts and people's relatives the likes of which I had not heard since adolescence. Then he reached for his coat and put on his shoe.

"Please don't quit on my account," I said. "I am but a guest."

"Aren't we all?" said the little man. He came over to me and bowed:

"Wolfgang Mozart at your service."

"Lorenzo Da Ponte," I said.

"Good God! Another Italian!"

"If we were in Italy," I returned. "I would exclaim 'Good God, another Austrian!'"

The little man laughed. "Yes. Things are topsy-turvy nowadays. Even billiard tables are awry. Hell, I usually make that shot drunk! I understand you've been made new court opera poet. I've been here in Vienna for two months and haven't gotten a decent commission, much less the Emperor's blessing."

I was startled by Mozart's train of thought. He conjoined the possibility of his making a shot while drunk with the fact that I had been appointed to a post. The fact that he knew anything about me was in itself not surprising: in Vienna everyone knew everyone else's business; art and politics were inseparable.

"That's probably because you're not one of us," I joked. "Not an Italian."

"I've nothing against the Italians. Except their music. A lot of noise and simple tricks. Presto followed by Adagio or Largo if they're really daring. A "forte" followed by "piano". Schoolboy stuff."

"Do you have some particular Italian in mind?"

Of course, I was being disingenuous here. I could have guessed his nominee, but I held back.

"Take Salieri, for example," he said. "That darling of the Emperor. At first hearing his music is impressive but when you listen carefully you hear it for what it is. Just brass and drums, drums and brass. No real substance. His "Cave of Trofonius" is like that. Just a lot of noise."

"And yet there are those who think Salieri a giant. I myself have done some work for him. You sound jealous, my friend."

"I am jealous. Not of his talent. God knows, that's little enough. But he has the Emperor's ear. He has influence."

"That's not a bad thing if he can help you."

"Yes, but he hasn't. Even faint praise would be something. Even a nod at the right time or in the right place. But Salieri is an Italian, so he is more politician these days than musician. Musically, he's a mere technician."

"Signor Mozart," I said. "I can assure you that being a mere technician is the best recommendation for entering the Emperor's service."

"Except for you, of course," Mozart said, smiling.

"Except for me, yes," I said. I was smiling too, looking him right in the eye.

We had been making our way out of the billiard room when someone hailed us from behind. One of the shirt-sleeved gentlemen approached us, still carrying his cue. In his other hand he was holding Mozart's wig and now held it out to the little man. Mozart took it, walked over to the mirror by the doorway and put it on.

From beneath it his blond hair protruded in odd wisps and shards, so that he looked as if he had but only recently escaped from a fire.

"The Emperor doesn't even know I exist," he said. "I could stand before him stark naked, my dildo hanging in the breeze, and he would never notice."

"But if he did take notice of that, dear friend, you could hardly expect to get a commission."

He laughed, and then walked back to the billiard table for a final look.

"Besides," I said. "The best way to get to the Emperor is by scratching his dog."

"You mean by curling up to one of his pets, like Salieri, for instance. No, Signor. Then I would become the dog of a dog. I had a chance to scratch him once. It was at a party given by Caffarelli. Salieri was there, surrounded by his fleas. I'm sure he saw me. I suppose he was expecting me to approach him and scratch his ear. I didn't have any music with me, but I carried a great deal of it in my head and could have played for him all night without it. At any rate I just couldn't bow and scrape and anyway it didn't matter. The great dog just turned away, taking his fleas with him."

"It's as you say, Mozart. Things are all awry in this world, more than just billiard tables. But what does it matter if you coat a man's vanity so long as you get the chance to show what you can do? I am not a politician, myself, but I have learned how to survive. Flattery by itself is no sin. In any case, don't be so severe with the likes of Salieri. He's a man of broad and authentic abilities. Besides, in the beginning of his career he, too, learned how to scratch the dog."

"Scratch, scratch," said Mozart, waving his arm. "Since you're so good at scratching, maybe you can put in a good word for me."

I suppose I should have been insulted, but somehow I understood that Mozart was only trying to take my advice, as difficult as it obviously was for him to admit it. I felt, in an odd sort of way, that he trusted me.

"There must be others," I said.

"I wish I knew them. Good shot!" he said to the gentleman who had given him his wig.

Once again we were making our way to the door. This time he paused as he observed a pianoforte in the corner. As if it were nothing more than a smaller billiard table, he leaned over the keyboard and began to play.

"Bravo!" I said. *"What's it to be?"*

"A miracle. Or nothing at all. Perhaps it'll grow into a symphony or shrink to a dance. I need money, my friend."

"Perhaps even an opera—to show the technicians," I said.

Mozart looked at me hard. *"Do you have something in mind, my friend? Something worth my time? Something that will pay, for the both of us, perhaps?"*

Mozart was charged as from a Galvanic current. In that moment we shared a mutual interest and sensed that collaboration was inevitable. He gave me his address—a frightfully expensive part of town for a struggling composer unwilling to scratch—and we parted.

"Don't forget," he called. *"When you get something worthwhile I can supply the music. It will be remarkable."*

Of that I had no doubt. By the end of the evening I had already conceived the idea for Figaro. As I departed for home I wondered whether Mozart had ever left the billiard room, or if he were still there, prone over the table even while the servants were putting out the last of the candles.

*　　*　　*

EIGHT

The Protégé
How Da Ponte introduced Mozart to
The Elector of Bohemia

Wolfgang Mozart to Michael Kelly   Kohlmarkt, September, 1787

Good old Kelly:

How I envy you in London. Your enthusiasm about the opportunities there has convinced me that I should have gone with you, especially when "Figaro" lost favor with the fickle Viennese. I am disgusted with the situation. "Figaro" is my best work, I can't do any better. Even Lorenzo, whose enthusiasm is usually infectious enough for both of us, even he is certain that we have produced something that should hold the stage for years. Everybody is singing "Figaro", nothing but "Figaro". Throughout the city the street musicians play it incessantly. One hears it while trying on a hat or wrapping up a herring. Yet I have gotten only 450 gulden for it, not another penny. This despite the fact that shitheads like Martini and others are reaping huge profits for work with which I wouldn't even wipe my arse. Obviously the Italians are running things there and Rosenberg, the court chamberlain, is under their thumbs. My papa, God rest his soul, had often warned me about composers having always to learn to sing for their supper. So all the praise and all the back-slapping and all the good wishes still keep me hard up to put bread on the table.

I should have listened to you, dear friend, and left for England. I remember having a delightful time when last there, but that was years ago when I was just a boy. The Italians hadn't quite gotten their grips on the musical establishment and the English were free to think for themselves. You'll forgive me, Kelly, if I say that the English for all their appreciation hadn't really understood opera, and probably never will.

Now, of course, it is impossible for me to go. I have been ill most of the summer, but I'm well enough to take on a few pupils. I have even finished a little serenade and some dances that should satisfy the public taste for diversion while putting some money in my pocket. Prague is a lively city, and if I can't be in London, I can think it no less a thing to be taking rooms here in the Kohlmarkt. Lorenzo arrived from Vienna last week and has found a place just opposite me. He runs over early in the morning, taking the stairs two at a time, knocking only once before rushing in.

"Good morning, little one." he says. "Let's go for some coffee and something to eat."

I put my finger to my lips and he understands by this that my Stanzi is still asleep, so he takes my arm and we descend to the coffee house. I'm sure you'll remember Lorenzo's appetite. It hasn't lessened a bit. We begin to talk about Bondini's proposal.

Do you remember Bondini, the manager of the opera house here? Aside from Lorenzo, he's the only Italian I can trust. He has promised to stage our next opera and Lorenzo had assured him in turn to come up with a libretto in less than a month.

You know Lorenzo's work habits, my dear Kelly,—or should I say `Ochelli, ha, ha!

When he was writing "Figaro" he would work as much as twelve hours a day, almost ignoring the ministrations of the sixteen year old serving girl who looked in on him hourly. Notice, I said *almost*. Lorenzo's appetites, as I've said, were as versatile as they were large.

"How can you deliver on your promise," I ask him. "Bondini is no fool." I knew that Lorenzo was already working on two librettos, one for that shithead Martini, and the other for Salieri.

"Business is business," he says. "I work in the morning for Martini, pretending that I'm reading Dante. In the afternoon I'll do Salieri's, thinking I'm studying Petrarch. For you, little one, I reserve the evening. You are my Tasso."

"Then by the clock you should now be reading Dante," I say. "And doing something for Martini."

You know Lorenzo. Like most Italians, he is something of a fraud. God knows, he does his share of posturing. I have lived and worked with Italians all my life, and have never known any of them who didn't carry themselves, even in their private moments, as if they were on stage or in the presence of some Cosmic Eye. Every one of them brings into the public arena his own sacramental notion of being kissed by Destiny. Every one of them is convinced that he's being observed, marked, noted, obliged therefore to live up to the expectations of fate and posterity. In this respect, Lorenzo is a true Italian. But he's also Lorenzo. It would be a mistake to dismiss his declarations as pure bravado. He would produce, all right, but on his own terms, with flare, and so you may be sure that on this occasion I took him quite seriously. Besides, there was never a libretto so bad that I couldn't do something with it.

Only once, in fact, did I find a book worthless, a deranged piece by Varesco called *The Goose of Cairo*. Papa—may he rest in peace—convinced me to write the score, and out of respect for him I went to work. My friend, that libretto was a real piece of shit. The climax was to occur in the second act when the long-presumed dead wife, now disguised as a gypsy, appears outside the walled city. She is bringing with her a large mechanical goose. She presents the goose, made in Cairo, you understand, as a gift to the prince, her husband. He is to carry the goose inside and leave it alone overnight in the garden. In the morning it will talk. Believe it, my friend. The prince certainly did. He accepts the gift from this woman, who looks vaguely familiar, and brings it into the city. Concealed in the belly of the goose is, naturally, the tenor. That night he proceeds to scale the tower and free his beloved. She has been held captive there by the prince, who now sees the wickedness of his ways and amends his life, etc. etc. As I've said, a real piece of shit.

But this brings me to the point of my letter. Lorenzo has an idea for a new opera. He broached it that morning over coffee. That is to say, *I* had the coffee, Lorenzo everything else. Since "Figaro" went over so especially well here in Prague, he is writing a kind of sequel, but in a more serious vein and about that rogue Don Juan. I like the idea and think I can do something fine with the character. As usual, Lorenzo is trying to keep the thing concise, and I rather like his instincts in this regard. It's too bad you're not here with us, kiddo, because there is a juicy part just right for you.

Yesterday afternoon Lorenzo came out on the balcony that looks across my rooms and shouted up to me: "Signor Mozart, I have a little something for you. Come up!"

I appreciate his peculiar scruples, by the way. He maintains a social delicacy by not calling me "little one" in public, but has no problem stepping out in full view and shouting up to me with a wine glass in hand. I am ashamed to admit it, but my first thought was that the "little something" he had for me was a cute little chambermaid, the sister, perhaps, of the one he has been ogling. I remember he once bragged to me how in Venice he had entertained—that was the word he used, "entertained", emphasizing it with an obscene gesture of his finger—how he entertained his landlady and her two daughters, simultaneously. Aside from the physical limitations involved in such an exploit, Lorenzo and Venice itself always gave me the feeling that anything was possible, but on this occasion I was both disappointed and surprised when I got up to his room to find him alone, sitting by the window, one leg thrown over the arm of his chair, his torso half turned, facing the writing desk. He was deeply intent, his quill carefully scratching across the paper.

"What have you got for me?" I said, imagining he had completed a scene from the opera.

"Just a minute," he said, tilting his head in admiration of the script. He smiled.

"Yes, it's perfect!"

I took the paper and sat on the chair. Lorenzo brought down his leg and leaned over me as I read. My friend, what do you think it was? The first act? A set-piece aria? If you made a pilgrimage to Mecca you wouldn't come close to a guess. So I'll tell you. It was a lengthy letter of recommendation, almost embarrassing in its praise. In it Lorenzo spoke of the "ravishing genius" of Signor Da Ponte. He went on to endorse the "elegant and transcendent workmanship" of Signor Mozart, his protégé. The two, master and protege will, let it be known, faithfully, honorably and profitably bring glory to whomever by these presents, etc. etc.

I suppose I should have been outraged, insulted, and righteously indignant. Papa, God rest his soul, would have posted Lorenzo as a scoundrel in every court. But that's not the worst of it. Here's the worst of it: the bottom of the letter carried a signature. Not Lorenzo's, of course. Not mine, naturally. It was that of the Prince, himself. The Elector of Bohemia!"

Lorenzo didn't wait for me to ask the meaning of it.

"Insurance, little one. You know how I despise politics. That's because politicians are stupid. No matter how good my poetry, or sublime your music, the powerful are just ordinary dolts and we artists need a cudgel just in case we have to beat some sense into them. A good word from a powerful friend is often more help than a head full of talent. Even if that powerful friend, like our elector, isn't aware of the aid he's rendering. It will not lengthen his stay in Purgatory, or keep him from going to Hell. Suppose Bondini fails us? Who's going to pay for our time? Our expenses? This wine, for example, do you have any idea what they charge for a single bottle? The Elector is our insurance, our cudgel, our bottle of wine."

I really should not have been surprised at all this. After we had met last year at the Baron's house—he has a wonderful billiard room, you know—I found out a few things about Lorenzo that would explain his practice. Among them was the rumor that he had forged a few letters of introduction to important people. That is how, according to some, he got his start. I can't vouch for these rumors. Having myself been the subject of not a few, I have cultivated an acidic distaste for the gossipmongers. But I saw what I saw.

Still, as Italians go, I'll take my chances with Lorenzo.

"What about your libretto?" I asked.

"Right here," he said, picking up a sheaf of papers. "I've got a good start on it. I'll bring you a draft tonight."

Sure enough, about eleven, I heard him bounding up the steps. This time he knocked, but only lightly, grazing the door as if by accident. Lorenzo knew I often did some of my best composing at night. Stanzi had gone to bed, and I was busy fleshing out some little phrases that I had jotted down in my notebook on the journey. Though still summer, the nights are cool in Prague. The first thing Lorenzo did when he came in was open the window.

"I've marked the places where the drama calls for music," he said. This is the way Lorenzo works. In most cases he has an unerring sense of timing and dramatic effect. Even in this first draft I saw no trace of that silly Egyptian goose. He's no Varesco, thank God. He likes to cut, to trim, so that at first glance he seems to have pared the life out of the work, but when I begin to compose for it I can see the musical opportunities his text has so slyly opened for me. Lorenzo himself is aware of such possibilities.

"See how I take care of you, little one," he says. "Maybe we really don't need his excellency, the Elector, after all."

Lorenzo is thinking of his libretto, of course, but he can be sure my music will not be wanting. I don't know what he intends to do with this letter, but I can't blame him for it. I have come to believe that he's right; that these days it often takes a friend, an Elector, if you will, to insure one's success. I can only wish he carried off his schemes with a little less passion. A clever, rich patron with a discerning ear is better than a prince who can't distinguish between a fart and a piccolo. Commend me to all my friends there. I must close now, as I hear Lorenzo tromping up the stairs, probably with a fresh idea. I hope it's not another letter this time recommending me to the KING OF ENGLAND.

Your friend,
Wolfgang

*　　*　　*

NINE

The Creditor
How Da Ponte became a capitalist

Manhattan Academy for Young Gentlemen

Mr. Da Ponte begs to inform friends and the public that he has opened his academy on Broadway Road where he will instruct young gentlemen in the French, Italian and Latin languages. Every attention will be paid to the morals of those entrusted to his care.

The notice in the *Daily Advertiser* made me nearly bust my britches. This fellow couldn't be the same Da Ponte who sold everything from battered hats and dried biscuits to old books and soiled ribbons from the back of a wagon and whose spavined horse nearly died on the road! He couldn't be the same rascal that borrowed ten dollars from me on the ship and who I thought I'd never see again!

We were twenty-six days out of London aboard the *Columbia*. I was on my way to New York to take over my brother's distillery business. I had struck up an acquaintance with a lean, wiry man with a face like a jeroboam—narrow and large of snout. At first he does little talking. For the first few days, the weather being pleasant, he strolls the deck, looking uneasy, scared, pale. But once the sea begins to roil, it being March and gusty, and the ship to heave like a man with a fever, he didn't come up at all, unless it was at night to take some air. Now as I recollect, I did see him seasick once, being tended to by a passenger, a widow woman. She was helping him puke over the rail, encouraging him to buck up. Have faith in the lord Jesus, she said, He will save all those who believe in him, amen, alleluia.

One day about three weeks out I see him topside, scanning the horizon. He's standing against the rail, one leg crossing the other, holding an elegant cane. I can see he's no American, his clothes had a sort of foreign cut and they seemed old and stodgy; He had the same worried look, as if he thought we were going to sail straight off the edge of the ocean. I've seen looks like his before, only they were mostly on fellows who were dreadful sea sick and were ready to puke on you if you so much as touched them. Just to be friendly I say good morning and ask if this was his first trip to America. He just keeps staring out beyond the rail and says that he had no idea how big the ocean was and that the poets had lied. I told him that the ocean wasn't all that big to someone who has crossed it as many times as I have. Not to worry, I say. The captain knows his business. The fellow looks at me with a limp expression, as if he had just taken a swim. The captain is more of a pirate than the Grand Turk himself, he says. He had paid forty guineas for his passage but then once at sea the captain tells him that his victuals were not included. He was forced, he says, to turn over his few belongings—some books and a set of spoons given him by some emperor—to keep from starving to death.

The fellow looks desperate, so just to be neighborly I ask him to sup with me, my treat, I say. I watch his face light up and he thanks me, bows, and grabs my arm. Then we go aft where the victuals are being served under a kind of tent. He obliges me first by eating two boiled chickens and by washing them down with a pint or two. He obliges me next by talking about himself.

I suppose that was his way of repaying my hospitality. He tells me that his name is Lorenzo Da Ponte and that he was a poet in the Old World but that here in America he is ready to do things the democratic way. What things? I ask. He doesn't really know, he says. But he thinks America is ready for his kind of services. What kind of services? I ask. He doesn't know, exactly; something, he says, where his talent can show the true measure of his genius. Naturally, I take that to mean something that would pay.

I don't need much assurance about his talent. I've seen fellows like him before. Many make this voyage expecting a new start but wind up arriving at the same old end. They travel light—no books or spoons—escaping some debtor's prison or the clutches of some penniless old hag suing for breach of promise. Somehow I don't see this Lorenzo Da Ponte as fitting that kind of mold. He had a way about him, a manner that declared he was a good, honest whiskey, no sugar or water added.

I tell him that I was taking over a distillery in New York and he seems interested.

His eyes widen and his body comes to attention, like he's just seen George Washington pass in a parade. He had heard that New York was a booming town and that very likely it would boom even bigger than Philadelphia and more important, and he thought he might get a living there. As for being a poet, he don't see that line as a way of turning a profit; it never did pay very well in Europe, he says, and it likely won't buy his bread here in America. I point out to him what he said about wanting America to appreciate his talent and he smiles. Yes, says he. That is true. But the mind can be fed only after the belly is full, says he. A man has got to eat before he can think. He learned that much as a poet over there. Then he looks me in the eye and cocks his head. By the way, says he. How is the distilling business, and what do you have to do to get into it? I don't wish to get too direct with him, after all, business is business and you can't really be too careful about sharing family secrets. I tell him that you first have to start with the right grain. You take New York, I say to him. Now New York has some of the best corn and some first rate barley, and you don't have to go too far to have it milled. Of course, that wasn't really telling him anything, but the way he looks at me and shows how interested he is you would have thought I was opening the Sacred Book and revealing the secret of the *Spirits*.

Then it happened. To this day I can't figure what went wrong, or for that matter if anything *did* go wrong. I'm not a man easily caught; I know which way the wind blows. But in this case I get the feeling I been had. Here's what I mean. I was telling him harmless stuff about the distilling business, like I said. Suddenly he puts his hand on my shoulder and looks me right in the eye. I'm glad we had this little talk, says he. You make me feel good about myself. It's a pretty lonely business taking up your roots and coming to a fresh New World says he. Especially when you get cleaned out by a pirate who calls himself the captain of a ship. I re-assure him, he says, that things will be all right in America and that Americans are a decent, generous folk, not like that Captain who had greedy designs on his purse, he says. That Captain gives Americans a bad name. I wonder, says he, if I could impose on our new acquaintance and rely more securely on your good wishes. Then he takes up his cane and shows it to me. It would be an honor to call you a friend, says he, a friend as generous, as trustworthy and as confident in my talent as the fellow who give me this stick. And now that I think on it, there must have been some magic in that stick. Maybe that stick was enchanted because I was being carried along by the man's palaver.

If you want to prove your regard and your faith in me, he says, if you want to show that you are as generous an American as that filthy Captain was a scoundrel, says he, I would be honored to accept a loan.

Now like I said. I know which way the wind blows. But it was like I had no power to resist. It was like taking a drink or two, and you still got all your senses and you know you're not drunk but you just don't give a damn. The upshot was I give that Da Ponte ten dollars and by the time we made landfall I regretted it, knowing for sure I'd never see him again.

But I was wrong. A few months later I was across the river in the Amboys on some business. I was just leaving a tavern when I see this wagon coming down the road. It had a worn, flapping canvas, full of holes across the top, as if it had been through the entire war of Independence. It was being pulled by a horse all lame and weak in the withers. I could see the whites of its eyes and the suds in its mouth as it strained to pull its clattering load over the last few feet of rise just above the tavern yard. The jangle that wagon made, the clanking and rattling of chains and glass and tin, reminded me of the noise of a theater troupe I once saw coming into town when I was a boy, except here there was no drum beating or people shouting, only the wheezing of the horse and the sharp whistle of the driver as he snapped the reins and threw a handful of pebbles onto the poor beast to encourage it. I couldn't recognize the driver, but he seemed to recognize me because he shouted and waved one arm in the air. I didn't have time to digest my surprise when I hear him say, How are you, my dear friend? We could not meet at a more opportune time. Yes, I say, coming around. Where's my ten dollars? Da Ponte gets down. He is wearing the same duds as on the ship, but they're all dusty and wrinkled, like he was sleeping in that wagon on a regular basis. As you can see, says he, sweeping his arm about, I've become a democrat and a capitalist. You got my ten dollars? I say, shaking his hand. My friend, says he, I never shirk a debt. I have been meaning to seek you out, but my business, as you can see, has kept me constantly on the move. But we are well met now. Come, says he, let me return a favor, and taking me by the arm he whirls and we go into the tavern. We sit down to a pint or two and some victuals and when the bill come he insists on paying. I notice how he scans the paper, closely studying the reckoning as if it was a state document. All this time, though, I can't get comfortable, thinking that somehow my ten dollars was the basis for his business and anyway I had just come out of that tavern and was pretty well full up.

Just like on the ship, he does most of the talking. This is his last run, he says. He has found some American patron and is ready to use his talents for the benefit of his new country. How about using your talents for my benefit? I say. Ten dollars. He smiles, and once again I find myself going his way. My friend, says he, I haven't got your ten dollars now. I am in the process of liquidating my business. Here he points to my ten-dollar horse and wagon cluttering the yard. I wish to discharge my debt honorably, he says. Yes, I say. But when? Ten dollars is as good now as later. I have a situation, he tells me, in New York. My Maecenas has been generous with me. If you will be so good as to visit my academy in a month's time I can and will pay you every cent. Here he gives me a card:

"Dr. Lorenzo Da Ponte, late of his Majesty's service: poet, scholar, pedagogue extraordinaire"

In the meantime we have left the tavern and he is walking to the back of the wagon. I see him take down the hatch. He reaches inside, his fingers fumbling amidst a pile of colored rags and things, and finally fetches up an old piece of cheap ribbon that looks as if it had once been fashioned into a cravat. He brushes it with his fingers, trying to bring it back to life, but it lay in his hands like a dead tongue. Da Ponte purses his lips and shakes his head. Then he reaches back into the wagon and pulls out a book with a stained cover. He puts the ribbon inside the book and walks over to me.

My good friend, he says. Let me give you something as a token of good faith. Please keep these with you and value them as I have. This book of sermons by the Reverend Josiah

Humpfnagel has been a constant solace to me over these many months. I now place it in your safe keeping until I see you next and can fully repay you.

Now I'm as religious as the next fellow, more or less, and I don't need no preaching on the art of keeping a tidy life. If it was a book on keeping a tidy business, that would be much more to the point. Morality these days is a matter of common sense, and that's why I can't understand how I could lose not my soul but my common sense when I give that Da Ponte fellow that ten dollars. Like I say, maybe that stick was enchanted. It must have put a spell on me, what with all the words, words, words spilling out of his mouth, one hand on my shoulder, the other holding out the book. And I like a fool taking it and almost thanking him.

All the while he's talking he is mounting his wagon. I watch as he goes down the road and disappears around the bend. I have been meaning to look him up and letting him make good his offer, but my own affairs have been keeping me fully charged and I never did catch hold of him. But one of these days I'll stop by his academy, like he says, and collect what he owes me. I won't expect any excuses then. There will be no more surprises. Like I say, that notice in the newspaper made me nearly bust my britches.

*   *   *

TEN

The Pupil
*How Da Ponte brought his students
to the glories of Italian literature*
(From the *Daily Advertiser*):

Table Chatter:

*Our Friend and Correspondent Mr. Jedidah Doodle reports that
Dr. Lorenzo Da Ponte has recently concluded his Peregrinations round
and about distinguished European Capitals and to our good Fortune
has deigned to settle in our esteemed Metropolis. Largely through the
good offices of Mr. Clement Moore, our signor has taken rooms on
the Broadway road where, we are told, he has already crowned his
Perambulations with the Establishment of an Academy for young
Men eager to drink from the intoxicating cup of the Muses. For the
sum of two dollars weekly Dr. Da Ponte will instruct his charges on
the Arts of Poetry, Literature and Declamation, and we understand
from Jedidiah that the entire City is agog, anxious to plumb the
depths of the signor's vast intellect . . . .*

He was a real cracker, that Da Ponte. At first I wasn't at all
pleased when I learned that my father had decided to enroll me

in the academy. I had already gotten my fill of so-called masters, most of whom weren't worth the twenty dollars per annum spent on forcing us to write out Latin cases and declensions. One pedagogue in particular used to sit at his desk brandishing his pointer, droning on for an hour his amo-amas-amats until his waistcoat raveled up the pink wattles of his belly, his eyes glazed over, staring into the back wall in some unseemly reverie. By the end of the term, so far as our Latin was concerned, we had learned only that Caesar knew the cause of war, expressing that fact in a crude pun, as a perturbation of the bowels.

Perhaps it was because of these kinds of masters that my father was so insistent. "I've heard good things about this Italian," he declared. "The Moores are convinced that he'll bring us up a notch or two." Still, as I've said, I had my doubts. So I wasn't expecting much when this crooked old fellow with no teeth but a headful of energy stormed into the little sitting room, laid down his walking stick as if it were a gauntlet and introduced himself as a gentleman, a great poet and an American, in that order. His energy, his enthusiasm was like nothing we had ever seen. If anything, this Dr. Da Ponte would at least be amusing. Here was a man who never sat still. His mind—never fixed on the back wall as was that of Master Amo-Amas-Amat—seemed established on something that lived and flourished beyond our ken.

There were at first only eight of us—Dolph DeGroot, Kyle Delafield and I formed the founding triumvirate—but even so the little sitting room which served as our first lecture hall was always cramped with books, papers and assorted goods. The space was almost claustrophobic, especially when Da Ponte went through his declamations. At these times he would roam among us, reciting, intoning, and sometimes even singing, so that the room shrank to physically suffocating proportions while in our minds it opened to luscious prairies of sound and light and form that we had never before experienced. There didn't seem to be any order to his presentation. There didn't appear to be any scheme or syllabus. There was only a spontaneous magma of sound and rhythm. Information was incidental, facts only way stations at which the mind could rest momentarily before rising again and mounting the surge. Strong, clear and dramatic, his voice rose and fell as the natural topography of the landscape. He taught us that learning a language and its literature was not a matter of rote, but a quality of "surrender", as he used to say. "You will drill on your own," he said. "We are not technicians. My duty is to make you surrender to the language, to capitulate to its sound, its color."

If there was a weakness in the Da Ponte method it was surely that the master often forgot that it was *we* who were paying for the privilege of declaiming and not the other way round. He was regularly caught up with his matter and when the muse was particularly seductive he bore on, barely stopping to hear, correct or encourage us.

He was at ease in a number of languages and was unprejudiced toward any of them, although Italian was naturally his favorite. One time, I remember, he asked us to recite from Tasso's *Arminta*, the first act chorus on the Golden Age:

> O bella eta dell 'oro,
> Non gia perche di latte
> Se'n corse il fiume e stillo mele il bosco:
> Mal sol perche quel vano
> Nome senza soggetto
> Quell'idolo d'errori, idol d'ingamo . . .
> Non mischiava il suo affanno
> Fra le liete dolcezza, De l'amoroso gregge.

After we had butchered the translation, Da Ponte began to correct us, which meant of course rendering his own version: "O, lovely Golden Age, not just of rivers flowing with milk, or honey dropping from the woods, but of the unborn shadows of treachery and deceit, not yet darkening the natural sweetness of mankind." Then he continued to quote beyond our passage, while we sat enthralled, surrendering, as he said, to the spell.

One of us asked him if there really was a golden age and if he believed what many of us had been told from the pulpit and the breakfast table that America was, indeed, the place where it was to begin. Da Ponte shrugged, and rested his walking stick on his shoulder.

"The poets don't lie," he said. "Poets are not interested in facts. Facts cannot tell us that there was not a golden age, or that there was. As for America, there is no past, no history, and no record of war or disease that darkens its land. Perhaps, then this *is* the place. I don't speak, of course, of morality or ethics or politics. The poets are not concerned with those, either."

And that was as clear or definitive as he ever cared to be on the subject. Even now, I can't say whether Da Ponte was being evasive or hieratic; whether he really drew a distinction between the reality of the poets and the experience of the rest of us who must get by on hard work, a little luck and an unflagging capacity for practical deceit.

A suggestion of an answer came one day a few months into the term. He was in the midst of a lesson when Eli the porter cum butler-cum maintenance man came in and whispered in Da Ponte's ear. It must have been an urgent or terrifying message because Da Ponte excused himself and quickly went out, leaving behind his impressive walking stick. This was something we had never seen him do. From the very beginning he had always carried his stick, sometimes cradling it under his arm, sometimes laying it on his shoulder, sometimes propping it behind him and leaning on it as if it were a third leg.

Now it lay on the table in front of us, its remarkable handle gilding the room, perhaps, as it seemed to us, a token of his own golden age. Some of us went up to the table to get a better look at it, as if it were some rare device, some mysterious totem, a kind of *sanctum sanctorum*.

Then we heard someone talking in the hall; it wasn't Da Ponte, but a crass, masculine, unfinished voice. We heard it say something about finally tracking down the good doctor and something about ten dollars and then we heard Da Ponte, muffled, as if trying to whisper, telling the voice that it shall have the money forthwith. Then there was silence and a few minutes later Da Ponte came back in, looking flushed. He picked up his walking stick and continued his lesson as if nothing untoward had ever occurred.

One of us asked him about his walking stick. Da Ponte glanced at it admiringly.

"It was a gift to me while I was in the service of his Majesty, the Emperor Joseph. I won't speak of those times. You are too young to appreciate their wonder."

The real wonder for us was how Da Ponte managed to keep the academy afloat, awash as it was with the periodic tide of sheriff's men who would often arrive in the midst of a lesson and abruptly, silently, carry off a chair or japanned box or ormolu clock. A few days later the things would be back in their accustomed places. We were never able to learn how the old master managed to redeem them, but one day we did get a closer look at the workings of such transactions.

Da Ponte was in the middle of a discourse when a knock on the door was quickly followed by the entrance of the sheriff, holding papers of attachment. Without waiting—he knew the rules by this time—Da Ponte went up to him and took the paper. "These notes are not due," he said.

"They been sold", the sheriff said. "All I know about it is that the fellow takin' 'em over is callin' 'em in. He wants his money or payment in kind."

"Who took over the notes?" Da Ponte asked.

The sheriff looked through his papers. "A gennelman named Taylor. Rufus Taylor."

"He is a rogue and a scoundrel," Da Ponte said.

"That's not for me to say," the sheriff said. "Maybe he is, and maybe he ain't. But he's the gennelman what's got 'em now and he has his rights."

"The money is not due yet. He'll have to wait."

"I'm sorry," the sheriff said. "All right, Frank. Go ahead."

The man named Frank suddenly swooped in and helped himself to a pair of sconces on the wall. Putting them under his arm, he looked around for some other prize that would fill his empty hands. He spotted a fine edition of Tasso on a cheap deal table, but if Da Ponte feared the loss of this volume he need not have fretted very long. Frank simply picked up the book, put it on the floor and grabbed the table.

At first we became accomplices in the act of saving Da Ponte's books from the depredations of the likes of Frank. When we saw him about to pounce on what we thought would be a book, each of us grabbed six or seven tomes from the shelves and put them by our chairs, as if they were ours. But we needn't have worried.

Over the course of the year we discovered that, indeed, books were the safest commodity to keep out of the hands of these "debt men" as we called them. Because they preyed on more valuable goods like a silver-plaited letter-opener or a filigreed handkerchief, the debt men let alone Da Ponte's library, although we knew that sooner or later, when everything else was gone, the books, too, would be swept up like so much flotsam.

We discovered, too, that Da Ponte was running up more debt by investing in gins that would produce artificial cotton or buying shares in offshore distilleries that operated aboard abandoned Dutch frigates. These were mere rumors, of course, but their frequency and improbabilities only lent them more credence, bolstered as they were by Da Ponte's frequent claims that he had become an American and a democrat.

In the end, Da Ponte's academy survived. The sheriff's men were somehow satisfied, and Rufus Taylor, apparently a man of some influence, never again interfered with the workings of the school, though most of us assumed that some day there would be a reckoning between the two men.

When it was time for the founding triumvirate to move on, we did so with only mild regret, our memories still green, alive with the image of old Da Ponte, his walking stick aloft, reciting from his own works and those of the other great poets.

So esteemed is this distinguished Signor, Dame Rumor has it that he will be inducted into one of our City's most influential literary Societies, whose Portals, we regret to say, have been closed even to our Correspondent.

Dr. Da Ponte is a handsome Man whose eyes gleam with Wisdom and fine Discernment. Jedidiah declares that the good Doctor cuts an imposing figure as he punctuates his Remarks with a brilliant Flourish of his Walking Stick, like the very wand of Apollo itself.

Those wishing to quaff from the Cup of the Muses may enter their sacred Precinct at No. 29 Broadway Road. We understand that when not imparting the Wisdom of the Muses to his Acolytes, the good Signor may often be found sipping the Ambrosia of the Poets in the Bookshop of Mr. Riley, the Irishman, also on the Broadway Road . . . .

*   *   *

ELEVEN

The Second
How Da Ponte came to fight a duel

When DaPonte asked me to be his second in that strange affair on Staten Island I could hardly be blamed from initially declining. After all, I hardly knew the man, having been introduced to him only that evening in our clubrooms. Besides, his grievance with Taylor had nothing to do with any of us, at least at the outset. Da Ponte had been gnawing on that bone long before he had come to America, and as far as any of us were concerned the matter between him and Taylor was for the Old World and should have been duly left behind.

Da Ponte was presented to us by Clement Moore, one of our most enthusiastic members. I like Moore. His enthusiasm is all the more genuine because it is the product of deliberation rather than spontaneity. Clement acts only when he has parsed the matter out, like a Latin subjunctive; and then he moves fearlessly. So when we saw this Da Ponte being escorted on Clement's arm, as is customary with inductees and their sponsors, most of us were already convinced of his rightness. Most of us, that is, except Taylor. He himself had joined our literary group only a few months before. He had been a theater manager in London, and I understood that he took great pride as an impresario who gave posterity a chance always and everywhere to bless his name by seeing and hearing some of the great actors of the world. Who these people were I never learned, but I must confess that he should have included himself among a host of third-rate thespians, for his self-praise and puffery were obvious signs to me of his limitations as an artist and a man.

As for Da Ponte, there was also a quiet self-assurance in his manner, but the contrast between the two men was distinct. Taylor was tall, wiry, and frenetic. He gave the impression of being incessantly busy: his joining our group was, on his part, a good deed rendered for our benefit rather than his, as if, God bless him, he was doing us a favor. He always wore black, as if to emphasize the serious aesthetic value of his presence. He unfailingly voiced an opinion in every circumstance, in every discussion, invariably prefacing it with allusions to his legion of literary connections:

"When I was in London I did this . . . When last I spoke to Coleridge he told me that . . . As my good friend Sir Walter—we call him 'Scotty'—once said to me . . ."

For myself, I cannot understand why so many of my fellow clubmen are taken in by this humbug. They almost lionize him, hanging on his every word as if he were Moses come down from the mountain, deferring to his dictates even in such matters as the kind of pictures hanging on our walls.

"A landscape is a most hideous fabrication," he would tell us as we sat (some of us) enthralled at his feet. "A hunting scene, too, is a vile imposture on the sensibilities. No, the only true kind of painting for the literary man is a still life. Nothing so inspires the ensemplastic imagination as a luscious bowl of fruits."

A few of us, like Clement Moore, remain civil to but properly inoculated against this Taylor infection. I would venture to guess that Moore's support of Da Ponte here was as much a counter to Taylor as it was an honest attempt to pump new blood into our narrow veins. Ironically, Da Ponte himself was hardly young.

Nothing was new about his clothes, certainly, and there was, in fact, a kind of creakiness about his demeanor: the rusty politeness of his bows, the studied English with only a trace of Italian accent, the walking stick resembling a sword by his side. I imagined him for an instant as a kind of knight-errant. Perhaps, indeed, that was the image that Moore saw: Da Ponte as a champion, tilting against the humbuggery of the world according to Taylor. On the whole, there was an air of quiet dignity about him, self-assurance, as I've said, that seemed to guarantee an honest dollar for an honest day's work. No wonder Clement was so keen on the man. The real wonder was how the two oddly complimented each other: the one young, ardent, aglow as if the guardian of some magic elixir; the other, confident, reserved, as if in possession of the secret.

I was the first to approach them to offer my congratulations. Clement was ebullient. "Leonard," he began. "This is the gentleman I had spoken to you about, Signor Lorenzo Da Ponte. Signor Da Ponte, this is Mr. Leonard James."

Da Ponte bowed and looked at me quizzically, as if trying to recollect where or when we had ever met. Perhaps I reminded him of someone. In any case the look passed quickly from his face and we shook hands. He had a remarkably strong grip for someone who appeared so frail. I know now that his frailty was but an illusion, suggested by the man's narrow, shrunken face, counterpoised by a rather importunate nose. He moved with an easy grace and had really little need for the walking stick that was his constant companion. I smiled back at him but had no chance of continuing the conversation, as Moore caught him up and bore him away. I watched as Da Ponte bowed to each member in turn. Then I noticed his back stiffen and his body harden as he reached the spot where Taylor sat—far be it for Taylor to rise! He treated all new members—those not his own inductees—as intruders; and Da Ponte, on this occasion, it seems, was an unconscionable trespasser. Taylor not only kept his seat, but also turned his body in the chair in order effectively to turn his back.

Taylor's incivility did not go unnoticed. Even William Dunlap, as gregarious a fellow as ever lived and one of the most forgiving of men, even he was shocked by Taylor's deportment. Da Ponte himself was polite but cold. He did not bow, did not take Taylor's hand (indeed, Taylor had never offered it), did not betray any emotion, though his eyes and taut lips were expressive enough.

Clement must have sensed the tension. He put his hand on Taylor's shoulder as if to say, "Pray, don't get up" (little chance of that!) and moved Da Ponte along. For a moment Da Ponte was unwilling or unable to move. For a second he stood above Taylor, fixed as though about to speak and I received the preposterous notion that he was about to strike the seated man with his stick. But the next moment Da Ponte yielded to the pressure of Clement Moore's hand on his arm and walked on.

His last stop was at the chair of J.C. Peavy, our Club's "poet laureate." He always had a verse or two available for any occasion. Everyone liked him and indulged him, knowing full well that the criticism he so ardently sought was really a disguised wish for praise. For years he had been working on what he called an American epic poem on the battle of Long Island. He was to call it, "The Conquest of Brooklyn Heights" and was keeping us posted weekly on his progress. At present he was well in the throes of Canto the Third which, he informed us, begins:

> Now chant, O Muse, of Freedom's native son
> The peaceful warrior, General Washington,
> Who left the plow, as Cincinnatus had:
> Now there's a man to reckon with, by Gad!

"Notice," he would say. "Notice how I've changed the hackneyed 'sing' to the more august 'chant'. What do you think, gentlemen? What do you think?"

For all of his poetic ambition, there was not a jealous bone in Peavy's body. He welcomed Da Ponte with a genuine effusiveness that virtually embarrassed the old signor. Meanwhile, Rufus Taylor sat thrumming his fingers on the arm of his chair, looking bored and annoyed.

Moore and I were not alone in perceiving that things were crooked between the two men, but nothing further occurred that night or for several meetings thereafter. As usual, we continued to enjoy our literary evenings, basking in the quietude of accepted opinions and common ideas. Occasionally someone would bring up politics, naturally disrupting our peace, as when some wag voiced support for the proposed grid that our city fathers endorsed for the laying out of our streets and avenues. Clement was particularly against it. "It's wholesale butchery'" he said, "economic execution, I tell you. They'll not pinch Chelsea into squares and rectangles."

One day I happened to run into Da Ponte coming out of Riley's. He was on his way to his academy but was genuinely pleased to see me.

"Good morning, Mr. James," he smiled. "Shall we walk together?"

"With pleasure," I said.

"I've been meaning to thank you for your warm reception of me at the club. It has been quite a while since I've had the pleasure of meeting such a stimulating group. Not since my days in Vienna have I been able to indulge in *conversatione* with men of such stimulating wit and with a deep appreciation of literature and the arts."

Meanwhile, we were nearing his academy. I could just make out the graceful lines of its façade as we approached. It was one of the few brick buildings in the neighborhood, an attractive two-story structure owned by the Moore family. It struck me that the building had just the right aura, if that's the word, just the right air, as the working residence of a man from whom we expected something wonderful. None of us, I suspect—not even Clement—would ever fully comprehend what that something wonderful could be.

We had fallen into a silence and I sensed that Da Ponte was waiting for me to say something when he halted. I could feel his grip tighten on my arm and I heard his stick tap abruptly on the stone. Across the street, coming out of the printer's shop was Rufus Taylor. I knew immediately that Da Ponte had seen him before I did. Taylor had apparently seen us, too, but he crossed the street as staunchly as a creditor and approached us with that swagger of his. He was folding a piece of paper, slipping it into his pocket.

"Good day," he said, not looking at Da Ponte. "You're luckily met. I have been meaning to bring up something at our last meeting but you have been so lustily engaged with the new people that I've deferred it in favor of the right moment, one more in keeping with its importance." He glanced at my friend, and then: "I wonder if you would be good enough to chat with me a moment about it. I'm sure your friend won't mind. As you know I've been in touch with my associates in London and I think I'm about to execute the cultural coup of the season."

"Really, I don't think this *is* the right moment," I said. "My friend and I are already late." I hoped Taylor would not see through my lie.

With this the man smiled and put his hand on my shoulder. "Of course, of course," he said. A prince, he deigned that I wallow in his generosity of spirit.

As soon as he was gone—having made only the slightest suggestion of a bow and not once acknowledging Da Ponte—I turned to my friend. His face had hardened, but it was softening now as we continued on our way.

"That really wasn't the time or place," I said.

Da Ponte puffed out his breath in scorn. "He knew that. He's a boor, but he's not stupid. He knew he was insulting me."

"What is it, exactly, that you two have against each other?"

"It's more what he has against me. But I don't wish to impose. Let me just say that our Taylor is an ignoramus."

"There are some us, signor, who share your opinion."

"Jealousy is something I can well understand and easily recognize," he said. "Vienna was a veritable university in the instruction of that vice. Taylor knows I despise him as a fraud. His prejudice is not so much an envy of talent—he knows I am greater than he—but of blood. He bears the injured vanity of the Anglo-Saxon, despising anyone born and bred south of Dover. He may tolerate Americans, at least when they are facing him, but he deems them below his contempt. That an Italian, a Venetian, should come between his shadow and the sun . . ."

"It must be rather awkward for you to put up with the likes of him baiting you, week after week."

"It's not his impertinence. As I've said, he's a boor, and at my age one learns to deal with his type. But it never ceases to amaze me that his kind do get on, even thrive, among men who should know better. I would have hoped that here in America we had forsaken the gaud and glitter of Taylorism and had finally understood for the first time in history the value of the true artist. Even at my age, you see, hope stays green."

"I could well imagine his 'cultural coup of the season.' What do you suppose it is?"

Da Ponte smiled. "A trained monkey, perhaps. Or worse, a third-rate soprano. My protégé would have relished the sight!"

"Your protégé?"

"Mr. Wolfgang Mozart. I was the one who introduced him to the glorious world of the theater. I gave his music, if I may say it, the poetic voice that so captivated the world, albeit for only a season or two. Mozart was the most inspired fraud-finder I have ever known. He could sniff out an artistic charlatan as surely as a pig its truffles."

"You know," I said. "You'll have to steel yourself against him when your turn comes to speak to our group. I'm sure he'll be at you that night."

Da Ponte nodded. By this time we had reached his academy and we shook hands.

"As surely as a pig its truffles," he said, and went in.

Da Ponte's turn to speak came soon enough. We convened, as usual, in the upper rooms of a large, airy building just off the Broadway Road, where the rent was much cheaper and the landlord more accommodating to casual occupancy and boisterous evenings prolonged by mild cigars, strong port and heady conversation. It was the second week since Da Ponte's induction. What he was to amuse us with we did not know. Most of us were pretty sure that he would discourse on his life in "literary" Europe. As for Taylor, he had been passing among us beforehand, proposing that the "Eye-tie", as he called him, would no doubt use the occasion to hawk groceries or used clothing or reconditioned hats.

More offensive was the man's surly confidence, an oddly peaceful kind of self-command by which he was convinced that he was right and that, perforce, we would soon be convinced of his rectitude. Taylor was a natural predator. He had no more compunction for behaving as he did than a fox devouring a chicken. When he sat down in his usual place he seemed, as I've said, oddly at peace. Moore came over to him and said something, but I couldn't hear, and Taylor's face gave no clue. As for Da Ponte, he had taken his chair on the platform, waiting for his turn.

"Gentlemen," said Mr. Dunlap, our president *pro tempore*. "I have the honor of presenting Mr. Lorenzo Da Ponte."

Da Ponte arose to our applause (ours, except for Taylor, of course, who sat glumly with arms folded and legs crossed, as if waiting to have a tooth pulled. I'm sure Da Ponte saw him, but he simply smiled, propped his stick in front of him and, resting his hands on it, looked directly at us. Without any introduction, without any commentary, he leaned forward, fixed his gaze and began to recite:

"Se vuol ballare, signor Contino
Il chiarrino le suonero.
Se vuol venire nella mia scuola,
La capriolo le insignero."

Then he proceeded to translate, now looking directly at Taylor:

"If you wish to dance, my dear Count,
I will play you my tune.
If you wish to attend my little school,
I will teach you a jig—you will never forget."

At this Taylor simply laughed, uncrossed his legs, stretched them out in front of him and yawned. But Da Ponte continued. Now he was explaining a scene from Tasso's epic poem, in which the prince of darkness assembles his army—the beasts and monsters of Hell—and urges them to attack the forces of the just. The fire of his imagination—Da Ponte's, I mean—had caught all of us by this time. Even Peavy, who usually took notes on every occasion, merely sat enraptured, forsaking any hope of finishing his own great epic.

But in the midst of Da Ponte's recital, Taylor rose from his chair, hooked his thumbs into the pocket of his waistcoat and, throwing back his head, emitted a scornful peal of laughter. He had waited for a lull in the presentation, a dramatic pause in the narrative that was to emphasize the coming clash of the armies. Its effect here was to bring forth a gasp from Dunlap, for it was obvious that the laugh was audible throughout the room.

Meanwhile Da Ponte kept on. Those of us nearest him could read the anger in his eyes, but we admired the discipline with which he continued. But there was no admiration from Taylor. He laughed again, more loudly, and yet again, reaching deep within to produce a hideous guffaw. Finally, he pushed his chair aside so that it grated harshly on the plain wooden floor. Then he tramped out.

There was little comment afterwards, I remember, and few compliments to Da Ponte. Most of us were still shocked and embarrassed. Taylor had deflected our attention just enough from Da Ponte's recitation so as to leave us numb.

A short time later, while sharing cigars and sympathy with Clement and Da Ponte, we noticed Rufus Taylor coming back in. As if nothing had happened, he began to work each of us, as if he were running for office, putting his arm around our shoulders, smiling into our faces, asking after our welfare. Da Ponte had been observing him, watching him while he oozed among us. I could well believe that the signor was irritated, jealous that Taylor had stolen his audience even now. He had been standing all this while in his place and now he raised his walking stick, as if in signal.

"Gentlemen," he continued. "One word more and I am done. Some of you have asked about my late friend, Wolfgang Mozart."

Now the fact of the matter was that none of us had ever asked him about this Mozart. Few, if any, even knew who he was. But I suspect that Da Ponte knew that Taylor would recognize the name and thus, in a way, he was out-Tayloring Taylor.

"He was one of the great geniuses of the world. I knew him well and introduced him to all the courts of Europe. I could tell you many tales about our adventures and would be pleased to regale you and your friends at a more opportune time at my academy. My library is at your disposal. I have the largest collection of Italian books in America. Some day I hope to enlighten you on the beauties of Italian literature."

"Beauties, indeed!" Taylor said. "Italian literature is small beer, to be guzzled only in boudoirs and prisons."

Da Ponte turned red. "You are more qualified to speak of prisons than I."

"I, sir, have never been to prison." Here he glared at Da Ponte.

"On the contrary," Da Ponte said. "The prison of the mind, the dungeon of the spirit, the keep of ignorance—these have been your perpetual preserve. You will be imprisoned all your life. And as for the boudoir, I'll admit you have little knowledge of that, unless it be the bedroom of a gentleman friend."

Here Taylor seemed to take a step toward Da Ponte, but Clement Moore quickly came between the two and easily deterred him. To be sure, Taylor did not press his move. He stood by calmly and watched as Da Ponte gathered himself and walked out. I thought now that that was the end of it. Da Ponte and Taylor, having made the most of their inevitable confrontation, would now live quietly as peaceful enemies.

But I was wrong.

Early one afternoon about a week later I was standing beneath our buttonwood tree on Wall Street when a young Negro whom I recognized as Bill Schermerhorn's boy came up to me with a note. It was from Da Ponte, wanting to see me. I stopped in at his academy late in the day and let myself in. It was the first time I had been inside and I was surprised to observe how cramped the place was. Books were everywhere—on floors, in corners, spraddled on the worn staircase that wandered up into a kind of hatch, even piled against a wall, propping up a picture. I found my way into the reception room—a parlor in better days, but now an after-thought, a garret filled with an odd assortment of tattered chairs and bruised tables, under which lay still more books. A bookcase adorned the far wall. Oddly, it housed not books but a collection of *things*: spools of ribbon, crushed bonnets, erstwhile kettles and jugs and some unlikely-looking creatures made of whalebone. The whole menagerie gave an unsettling shape to Taylor's remarks about Da Ponte's being a kind of rag man.

Suddenly Da Ponte himself came in, looking strange. Then I noticed that for the first time since I had met him he was without his walking stick. Without formalities, too—and I was glad that we were now beyond that stage—he motioned me to a chair.

"I need a second," he said.

"I can give you an hour, my friend. Even the rest of the day."

"No, no. He's challenged me to a duel."

"Who? Not Taylor?"

"Two of his lackeys approached me this morning demanding satisfaction."

"The man's an even bigger blockhead than I thought. It's *you* who ought to be seeking satisfaction."

Da Ponte smirked. "I'm satisfied enough that he's lost face. But he's been insulted and this is his way of retrieving it."

"You threw them out I hope."

His silence answered me.

"The whole thing is illegal," I said. "We'll have him arrested."

"Yes," said Da Ponte. "This is America. We are much more apt to settle things in the courts than in the field. No. Having him arrested will only demean me further in his eyes. Boors and imbeciles must be dealt with on personal terms. It's the only conduct they comprehend."

"Nonsense," I said. "You're going to ignore the whole thing."

"My friend, I can't."

"But he already knows you're not afraid of him. You've nothing to prove."

"If you refuse me," he went on. "I shall still go ahead. In the course of my life I've met the likes of Taylor many times."

Realizing I was making no headway with him, I tried a different tack:

"Does Clement Moore know of this?"

"I cannot impose any further on the good nature of my patron, or rather, my friend. He's already been most generous with me. No. If you won't act as my second, I shall proceed on my own."

At this point Da Ponte left me, the only time during our acquaintance that his manners had left *him*. But I understood his anxiety and forgave him.

During my walk home I considered the matter. For one thing, I could take my own advice about the duel and ignore the whole affair. But my friendship with Da Ponte, as young as it may have been, demanded more than my public indifference or private silence. Besides, I was not indifferent; I liked him, and that was warrant enough for my concern. I knew I could not stand by; I must do something. I could intercede for him with Taylor, but knowing the kind of man Rufus Taylor was I thought better of the idea. No, Da Ponte was right on that point: Taylor would only think the worse of him and make his membership with the club an agony of embarrassment or reproach. Going to Clement, on the other hand, would be presumptuous, almost impertinent, considering Da Ponte's avowed feelings about involving his benefactor. As for going to the police, that, too, was out of the question. The recent death of Mr. Alexander Hamilton had infuriated them: win or lose, Da Ponte would get only a hardened, vindictive justice.

I was in a box with but one way out. In the end I reluctantly sent word to Da Ponte that I would act as his second.

Knowing little about the so-called "code duello" I consulted a few old books on the subject, mostly translations from the French. These I obtained from Riley's, being careful to appear more curious than intent. Reading them I realized the magnitude of the burden Da Ponte had asked me to take on. If I were the least bit indifferent or careless, if I did not observe the most correct punctilio in performing my part of the ritual, I would endanger the life of the very man I was charged to protect. At the very least I was to give my man a fair chance of blowing out the other man's brains. Doubtless Taylor had carefully chosen his people. His character alone suggested his being involved in numerous duels before now. I was convinced that he was an expert. Certainly, he had to have been more adept at fighting a duel than in promoting art.

In any case, the arrangements were duly made. Taylor's second was a quietly pompous man who, I learned afterwards, was a failed actor, hastily exiting the Philadelphia stage amid volleys of hoots and apples, and who dangled at the end of Taylor's fob in the hopes of a professional resurrection in New York. This was the "cultural coup" about which Taylor had been so excited that day he interrupted us on the street.

The "vindication of honor", as the actor put it, was to be achieved on Staten Island, a quiet, hilly place at the outer edge of the bay where few people would notice and fewer even care. We landed on the beach on a chilly November morning. The sun was just coming up over the low hills of Brooklyn, and directly in front of us, about five miles off, we could see Manhattan and a few masts at the throat of the horizon. Huddled in their midst, just emerging from the dark, was the landmark steeple of Trinity Church.

Taylor's people were already there—his second, and another man, a short, over-fed fellow wearing a beaver hat who was introduced to me as "a surgeon of rare skill and rarer discretion". I did not see Taylor, but his second, the actor, looked at me with a woebegone face and expressed surprise that only I was accompanying "the dead man." I received a complacent smile when I asked if Taylor had not yet come.

I helped Da Ponte out of the boat and paid the ferryman. He was a sober-faced, dirty youngster who—despite the weather—wore only a white shirt with the sleeves rolled above the elbows and insisted we call him Commodore. Da Ponte's grip, I remember, was firm, strong, as he grabbed my hand and stepped onto the beach.

Almost at the same time, Rufus Taylor stepped out from behind a clump of trees, just fifty feet from us. He was dressed in a tight-fitting brown and gray surtout. I knew at once that he had chosen the outfit for its effect as camouflage. He had been standing there, apparently, all the while, only now becoming visible as he moved toward us. In his right hand he was holding a book, and as he walked he began flipping through the pages, as if our arrival had interrupted his reading and he was thus hastening to finish.

"Mr. Taylor has been perusing the Poets of Melancholy," said the second, earnestly. As if on cue, Taylor himself sighed, snapped the book closed and murmured:

"And all that beauty, all that wealth 'ere gave,
Awaits alike the inevitable hour:
The paths of glory lead but to the grave."

To which the second seconded: "Amen. Amen and Adieu."

Through all of this Da Ponte was unmoved. He walked to a level part of the beach and stood arms akimbo, as if waiting impatiently for his valet. It becoming evident to Taylor and his men that Da Ponte was not to be scared off, the second reached into a small portmanteau. Bringing out a red leather box he began walking toward us, carrying the box in his arms like a baby about to be baptized.

If it is true that one's life flashes before the eyes at the imminence of death, then truly an analogous revelation may come to one at other crucial moments, bizarre or otherwise.

For as the second walked toward us cradling the box, I fancied that I was watching my own butler carrying a case containing my entire legacy of silver-plated spoons, knives and forks, to be used on the occasion of this special feast. Rufus Taylor, his failed actor-cum-second and his discreet surgeon, would be lounging on the sand across from Da Ponte and me and we would be admiring the spoons. "What a lovely piece," Taylor would be saying, holding it up to the rising sun. "Amen," the second would say. "Amen and Adieu."

What was presented to us, of course, in the light of reality and the rising sun was a pair of dueling pistols. "A matched set of Mantons," the second noted. He was standing beside me, holding open the lid of the box. I noticed that the pistols bore the initials "RT." on their stocks. If I had harbored any doubts as to Taylor's experience as a duelist, they were gone now and for Da Ponte I feared the worst.

The rest was played out as if a dream. I seemed separate from myself, an onlooker, a disembodied spectator viewing the action in pantomime. I recall no sound, no color, only the silent movements of players having no lines, just gestures. I saw myself taking out the pistol and the pouch of powder and ball. I stood looking stupidly at them while Taylor's second took the other pistol and began loading it.

My hasty reading had included a short treatise on loading the pistol, but all my cramming of the subject fled now as quickly as my doubts that Da Ponte would be killed. I tried to recall the proper way of priming the powder into the flash pan and of dropping the ball into the muzzle. It would have been clever of me to steal a glance at Taylor's second to see how the procedure was done. I should have remembered that the code demanded that both pistols be loaded in full view of the combatants. But I was, as I've said, an inert being, a painterly observer, as on a picnic with my set of spoons. With his back to me the second loaded his man's pistol and I could do nothing but wonder if the wadding went in first, or not at all; did I use too much powder, or not enough? Do I ram the ball home after it is dropped, and how forcefully?

In the end I convinced myself that I had done my best, but was angry with Da Ponte because he had forced me into so much guilt, uncertainty and incompetence. He was standing now on level ground, near a copse of small scrub that divided the beach from the rocky hill behind us. He had taken his position and was waiting impatiently. Meanwhile, Taylor's second had finished and had given over the pistol. Taylor was standing not more than twenty paces from Da Ponte and had turned to face him.

But Da Ponte had already turned quizzically to me and I suddenly realized that I had been standing there all this time, the pistol still in my hand. Rather than presenting it to him, I had stood like a tree in a petrified forest.

I saw myself walking to him. My mouth was dry. Though I was wearing a coat I was shivering, but I don't remember being particularly cold. What I most distinctly remember, and that most emphatically, was a point that the treatise had made quite clear: the loaded pistol had to be carried with the muzzle pointed upward. Bravely I bore it thus to Da Ponte. "See," I saw myself as telling him. "I bring it to you pointing upward."

Da Ponte took the gun, not looking at me. I could not tell if he were frightened. He stood erect in the red frock coat he had borrowed and squared off, facing Taylor like a man ready to ask for a loan. Taylor turned sideways, presenting Da Ponte with a smaller target. Then he raised his left arm—his pistol was in his right hand—and brought it in front of his face, below his eyes, as if he were shielding himself with an invisible cape. He had not raised his pistol for a shot, and its muzzle, I was glad to see, was pointed upward.

But then the terrible thing happened. In colorless silence, in a kind of bizarre tableau, I saw Da Ponte momentarily lower his gun as he fixed his feet in position. The pistol was *not* pointed to the sky, but to the ground. According to the dueling books, he had committed a cardinal sin, and he was about to pay the price. For as I looked on in horror I saw the ball plunge out of the barrel of the gun and plop at his feet. Perhaps Da Ponte saw; perhaps he heard what I in my trance-like state did not. Still he gave no sign of hearing or seeing. Taylor might have, nay, *must* have seen. But it was already too late. In one continuous motion, Da Ponte raised the pistol, flipped it into his hand, and holding it by the muzzle, hurled it like a tomahawk toward Taylor's head. The pistol struck Taylor on his outstretched arm and caromed into his face, hitting him just above the eye. He yelped and fell on his back, his own pistol going off, and the ball hitting his actor/second in the buttocks.

The shot broke my trance, and I heard Taylor shouting, "I'm hurt. I'm hurt, God damn it". The actor merely lay whining, sprawled across the portmanteau. Near him, the discreet surgeon pronounced the injury as only an "arsenine" wound and giggled.

As for Da Ponte, he wrapped his coat more closely about him and called to me for help. He had, he said, bitten his tongue in throwing the pistol so forcefully. He feared that he would not be able to recite well enough the next time he was called upon at the club.

*   *   *

TWELVE

The Poet

How Da Ponte survived an epidemic

Mon. April 20

I had been excited all day with the prospect. Tonight was to have been my turn at the Club. After Da Ponte's encouragement a few weeks ago I had revised some passages of my epic and under a sudden burst of inspiration had even composed an additional seventy-three lines, leaving off with the sequence in which General Washington holds back a tear upon reading in a letter from Martha about the death of his favorite dog, Lucifer. I had been planning to read those lines, together with an earlier scene, and had rehearsed all afternoon. But I was to be disappointed. Dr. Francis, our secretary, asked to say a few remarks, and all of us could tell by his looks that something unpleasant was afoot.

"Gentlemen," he began. "This is not the time to talk of poetry or politics. I've got some very bad news. I've just come from a house over in the Five Points district, the Fitzgerald's. The whole family, dead."

He had been called in by a fellow doctor who wanted confirmation of his own diagnosis. The mother and her three children—the old man, apparently, had run off weeks before—lay in the back room. There were no windows, the candles had burnt down to stubs, and even on that bright sunny day he and Dr. Marsh had to go in carefully with lanterns. Dr. Francis told us that he detected the sweet, nauseating stench that he recognized immediately. Together the two men went over to the bed and pulled back the gray sheet under which the bodies lay, fully dressed except for shoes. Already discolored, their faces were pinched, as if hollowed out, their eyes half open. Even the children looked hundreds of years old. Their tongues, folded back into their gaping mouths, were chalky and swollen.

"No doubt about it," Dr. Francis had told his colleague. "It's the cholera."

One of us—I forget who—asked Francis if he could be mistaken; maybe this family's immolation was an isolated event. After all, the Fitzgerald's were Irish. Everyone knew how shiftless, ignorant and dirty they were.

Dr. Francis snorted. "It's the cholera, all right. We're in for it, now! My advice is to stay indoors. Drink plenty of brandy. I believe alcohol has some properties that can forestall the disease. Drink brandy. Plenty of wine, that's what I'm going to do. Douse your place with lots of vinegar."

For some of us Dr. Francis' prescription sounded the only benign note in an otherwise discordant evening. I have little doubt that the regimen will be religiously observed, especially since the dosage permits the patient the benefit of being his own doctor. For myself I felt little fear. I confess that I came away from the meeting almost elated. Here, at last, in my own lifetime, loomed a subject worthy of the noble collaboration with the muse of poetry. Must I admit to stifling a sense of guilt at my own depravity in seeking to profit from the love of the abominable? In putting aside my epic of the battle of Brooklyn Heights to take up the story of what Francis fears will be an epidemic, am I not a kind of cannibal, feeding off the flesh of human experience, coldly ruminating the unheroic remains of the Unspeakable? I have, at this very moment, devised a title: "The Fourth Horseman of the Apocalypse: or, Cholera in New York. By G. A. Peavy." Dare I draft a fearful Invocation?

> Come thou, 0 Muse, and whisper in mine ear
> The horrors and the terrors of that year.
> When corpses gaped with tongues all white in death
> And even goodly doctors held their breath . . .

April 22

More bad news. Doctor Francis was right. The cholera has stuck hard and often. Some of the older people have died even in their very doorways. One fellow was found dead in his privy, his thighs covered with his own filth and blood. Fear is the only passerby in the streets now. Every lane, every alley, even Broadway Road as far as Wall Street is nearly deserted. Mayor Hone has ordered the streets to be doused with vinegar, but workers are afraid to come out so that barrels of it line the curbs with no one to do the job. The streets are dark at night because the watchmen refuse to risk their lives to light the lamps

We hear of deaths in almost every home, at first in the Five Points district, but now the rumor is that even the Battery is not safe. From the start of this thing the best business in the city was Harmon, the undertaker. His carpenters couldn't make the coffins fast enough and there was no shortage of stout men to lug the corpses away towards Spuyten Duyvil where some say the bodies were dumped into the river and the coffins returned empty. Another rumor, probably. In any case that was early on. Affairs are different now. Today the undertaker can't find men to pick up, much less haul away, the dead. No one wants to risk it. Harmon has even placed a notice in the *Advertiser*. "I will pay a dollar a day," he declares, "to any man, able-bodied or not, who will redeem the deceased at his respective domicile and convey the remains to the emporium for preparation, or in some cases, to their appropriate resting place." He doesn't spell out the resting place, appropriate or not, but he does sweeten the offer by paying those who use their own wagons an extra fifty cents a head.

April 25

A few days later and still no takers on Harmon's offer. All except one, or rather, two.

I know this not from second hand but by my own experience. I was in the throes of my composition on "Cholera", etc. when one evening, just after sunset, the Muse suddenly left me and no sort of cajoling on my part—no scratching my head or sitting back in my chair and stretching my legs—could bring her back. Frustrated and restless, I put on my hat and doused my handkerchief with vinegar. Putting it to my nose, as instructed, I made my way across Chelsea down to Coentie's slip. No ship had docked, but there were two or three that lay at anchor in the bay, waiting for the quarantine to lift. From the present state of things I suspected they would have a long wait.

I proceeded across Water Street and began making my way towards Trinity Church, passing Harmon's funeral emporium on my left. Perhaps it was the quality of light that evening (there was no moon); perhaps it was the pervasive atmosphere of gloom and despair, but I was suddenly taken up by a startling apparition. I say "apparition" because what I saw contradicted all I thought I knew about the man working in the shadows before my eyes. Actually there were two men. The first was coming out of a doorway carrying what must have been a corpse wrapped in a winding sheet. He himself was wearing a dark apron, the kind often worn by a butcher or a tradesman, and he was carrying the front end of the body, the head braced under one arm, the other supporting it as he lurched sideways toward a wagon at the curb. It seemed to me I had seen this fellow around town. He was one of those curiously rootless men whose occupation is to graze among the streets sniffing out any carrion of opportunity. I had seen him often enough to consider him harmless.

But it was the other fellow whose appearance at this place, under these circumstances, made me gasp. It was none other than Signor Da Ponte. He was at the other end of the corpse, his hands cupped under its feet. His mouth was covered by a handkerchief, doubtless soaked in vinegar, but I recognized him well enough.

I had been standing on the corner, near Merchants' Bank, and I knew that Da Ponte and the other man couldn't see me. As I watched, the two men laid the body in the wagon and then went back into the building. A few minutes later they came out with another body, wrapped as its predecessor, this one considerably heavier because they lugged it to the wagon and heaved it in as if it were a sack of iron ingots. Then they closed the backboard and climbed into the seat. Da Ponte drove. It was then that I observed the horse's hooves were wrapped in cloth so that they made little noise.

It was an easy matter to follow them, especially since the wagon rolled only twenty or thirty yards up the street. It pulled up before a three storey edifice, the ground floor of which housed a haberdashery. The two men got out and entered the building, and I could hear loud crying and moaning from a third floor window. Someone yelled "No" and then began crying. Soon Da Ponte and his partner came out, once again carrying a body. This one had been hastily wrapped in what appeared to be a bed sheet. I think it was a woman. By this time Da Ponte had removed the handkerchief from his face. During this interval I was busily taking notes of what I was witnessing, but in the confusion of the evening I must have lost them, because I am now writing this from memory.

Freighted with the three bodies, the wagon made its way across the square to Harmon's. I saw Da Ponte get down—he amazed me with his agility—and knock on the door of the emporium. Harmon, a large fat man eternally dressed in a black frock coat, came out, looked into the wagon and said something to Da Ponte who in turn motioned to the man in the apron. Together they began unloading their cargo, Harmon standing beside the wagon, merely watching.

When the last body had been deposited at the emporium Da Ponte and his partner came out. The man in the apron climbed into the seat and grabbed the reins. Da Ponte stood beside Harmon. As if in some weird dumb show, I watched Harmon reach into his pocket and count out a specific sum into Da Ponte's outstretched palm. Then they shook hands, Da Ponte climbed aboard and the wagon rolled away.

As I sit at my desk now in my rooms, I wonder what to make of it all. Only a short time ago Signor Da Ponte was discussing literature and the creative process. He was encouraging me in my work, inspiring me to follow my imagination and temper it with discipline. He was my patron, urging me to continue courting the Muse. Yet here he was, lugging bodies on moonless nights, delivering them up to his own sort of patron and for his labors pocketing, perhaps, four dollars and some odd cents.

For the life of me, I can't figure it all out. Who is the real Da Ponte?

*　　*　　*

THIRTEEN

The Impresario
How Da Ponte brought Italian opera to New York

(Early Draft of Part Five of my Memoirs)

You who know me so well must not be surprised when I declare that the enterprise—if successful—would be one of the principal accomplishments of my life. Surely you must admit that in spite of reverses, despite the snubs of the powerful men and the jealousies of the little, despite the predations of thieves and scoundrels both at court and in the common street, despite countless removals from one country to another and from one continent to another, despite the chicanery of greedy sea captains and the importunities of impatient creditors, despite the difficulties of making a living in a new world—difficulties which a man of lesser spirit and baser abilities would find virtually insurmountable,—despite all these, no one could doubt my patriotism or my zeal for the promotion of Italian culture in my adopted country.

Having reached well beyond the Biblical allotment of three score and ten, I have lived to pursue two destinies. My first destiny was to bring to light the genius of Mr. Wolfgang Mozart. It was I who put bread on his table and glory in his name by providing him with the poetic inspiration, which he so wonderfully shaped into the finest operas ever seen. He died young, and it is a shame that in this country—*my* country, now that I have become a citizen—his name is so little known and my own contribution to his success has lain buried with him in some pauper's grave.

So it is that I come to my second destiny. It has been taking shape these ten years, during which I have established an Academy for young gentlemen, introducing hundreds, thousands, to the glories of Italian literature and culture. But I have not been satisfied. There yet remains the more rewarding achievement of bringing all my experience, all my abilities to bear in a validation of what has come to be my life's work: promoting Italian opera here in New York. I almost said "vindication", for there has been much in my past that I regret—omissions and commissions of all sorts. But they are part of that grit, that distillation which, at the end, rather ennobles life than besmirches it. A man should have no regrets while he still breathes, while he still has time to finish what he perceives to be his calling. And so, yes, bringing Italian opera to fresh ears and new eyes is a proper validation, worthy of a man who has lived as long as I.

Fame and glory aside, there is money to be made. If Spain has made millions plundering the New World of its gold, I, Lorenzo Da Ponte, now of the New World, could make a fortune mining the musical and dramatic riches of the Old—and so things come full circle.

Strangely, it was the onset of cholera that brought my second destiny closer to fulfillment. The whole city was under siege, like some latter-day Thebes under a curse.

Many of its citizens, the rich especially, and the shopkeepers, too, determined to flee. In a matter of days the town was eerily quiet. Gone was the clatter of the freight wagons and delivery carts. The cobbles along the Broadway road bore only the sounds of wooden coffins being hastily lowered at doorways. Above the closed shops you could hear moans or sobs, or someone vomiting. The smell of vinegar was everywhere. Even the horses that pulled the hearses wore feedbags doused in vinegar as they made their way, their hooves muffled in black, the coachman, poor fellow, bedecked in black and slouching in his seat, seemingly unconcerned, as he had brandied himself to the gills.

Tontine's was closed, and so was Riley's. It would be impossible to get the Italian books I had ordered. They would have been an extra source of income, as I sold them to my students. But I had no students now, not while the cholera abided. In Venice I remember days, even weeks, when a sodden pestilence hung like a stench in the very air, especially in February and March, when the canals gave off a strange lurid glow. Most Venetians went about their business, taking the disease as naturally as sunrise, trusting to fate and the inevitability of spring. Here in America we seem to operate always with a sense of alarm, as if the coming day were but a prelude to emergency. A philosopher might speculate on this peculiar penchant of Americans to think and to act as if always in the face of crisis. For myself, I am not so sure that this impulsiveness is not a result of a lack of a past, a lack of a sense of history or of consanguinity to place. But as a practical man I see it as a good thing. I know that I saw the cholera as a means, an opportunity.

And so I determined to leave New York for the time being. With no students to help me make a living, I closed the academy and struck out for New Jersey and Pennsylvania where both the air and the opportunity were kinder.

I was used to moving. I could hardly recall a period of a few months in the course of my life during which I felt the beatitude of comfort with a place. Before long, as the world goes, I would be victimized by jealousy, ignorance or politics, and find myself once more on the road. And as for that, Sudbury, Pennsylvania or Elizabethtown, New Jersey would prove no worse than Vienna or London or even New York when one was compelled to survive.

In these places, the cholera was but a gothic tale. Goods were plentiful and cheap and my experience in America had taught me that nothing was to be gained by being afraid. You will remember the ten ladies and gentlemen in Giovanni Boccaccio's *Decameron*, a work, I regret to say, which many Americans have not heard of but which I introduced to my students. To escape the ravages of the Black Death these ten fled to a villa in the Tuscan hills and waited out the disease by telling stories. On the one hand they exemplify humanity's heroic ideal: survive at all costs. On the other they personify the basic weakness of the mediocre: the inability to seize a greater opportunity from the mere act of survival. What, after all, does a man do once he has survived? Surely he cannot spend his life hiding in the hills, telling tales and waiting for better times.

The cholera, then, as I have said, was my opportunity. For the second time since coming to America I went into business. For the next two years I made a good living in several successful ventures and a bad living in several failures. A scurvy fellow who convinced me he knew the distillery business ran off with some money of mine and a bookstore in Sudbury turned out to be a bad idea in a town where not even the mayor could read or write. But by and large I survived, even thrived. Yet I sensed that my second destiny was at hand. In the midst of counting apples and measuring ribbon, among the stacks of worn hats and second-hand books, it called to me. It beckoned, as I weighed a pint of dry beans or cut a yard of yellow calico. At night, while I slept, it appeared to me, a certain vision of my true calling. It was clear; it was obvious, undiluted by the beguiling but fatal act of fleeing into the hills. Even establishing my academy had been a sort of flight. No, my true destiny, as I have said, was as champion of Italian opera.

Having shed the life of a peddler once and for all, I returned to New York with a simple plan. I understood how the thing was to be done. I still knew some of the best singers in Europe, and though it had been years since we last saw one another, I had been keeping abreast of their careers. I would simply write to them, partly on the grounds of sentiment, partly by the claims of old fellowship, but mostly, as I was to make clear, for our mutual financial advantage. There was also my good friend Michael O'Chelli. The three of us—he, Mozart and I—often celebrated together, quietly, you may be sure, and usually in some snug retreat where we could enjoy our just acclaims as singer, musician and poet in the peaceful calm of a dignified self-respect. Ochelli, to be sure, was always the most boisterous. For an Irishman he was particularly discerning in the matter of fine wines, and it was only through my own efforts that he refrained from celebrating too vociferously. I had heard that he had been in America a number of years ago. I may have read something about his bringing **Blue Beard** back to life, but our paths had never crossed and it is a pity that I never got to see him again. I suppose he knew that Mozart was dead. I would certainly mention the fact when I now wrote to him.

Clearly Ochelli would never venture to sing again. Age and a propensity to fat would disabuse him from even the vaguest hopes in that direction. Besides, I understood that he was enjoying a well-earned retirement somewhere in the south of England where, I heard, he was overseeing the production of a dry port from his private vineyard. Ochelli, then, would give me some names and some invaluable advice.

As for the others, theater managers, spurned patrons and the rest, I was surprised at some of their responses. Some professed to be themselves surprised, thinking I had been dead these many years. Several thought I was an impostor. Two asked me for money.

But by the time I returned to New York that fall I had received a letter from him. He included several names, singers whose reputations were still intact, although he doubted, he said, that their fame—or lack of it,—would matter much to an

American audience. One of the singers he recommended was Madame Pasta.

He had seen Giuseppina Pasta perform several times in Covent Garden. She had, in fact, played the princess in his *Blue Beard* and he liked her voice. In his letter to me he had particularly praised her performance in the mad scene, wherein she was called upon to rip out her hair and eat it in front of her lover. I confess I did not like the play. Though Ochelli's own voice is sweet and firm, as a dramatist he leans too much to the sensational and I would rather remain a silent judge of his ability, demurring in honor of our friendship. While affirming the quality of Pasta's voice, however, he would not vouch for the quantity of her flesh. Madame Pasta struck him, he said, as someone on the verge. She was not yet stout, but her overall amplitude seemed to be lying in wait, panting quietly amid her thick neck and firm, muscular shoulders. At any moment, on any occasion, perhaps just round the next engagement or within the span of her approaching birthday, her flesh would break loose, emerging as a kind of ferocious counterpoint to her delicate *vibrato*.

His recommendation came also with a warning. She would be worth engaging, but I would have to provide only the finest accommodations for her and her companion, a young man fresh out of his teens who served as her valet, her advisor and, it was rumored, as a kind of quartermaster—what we used to term "a serving cavalier"—for her more intimate needs. Additionally, the finest box had to be reserved for her, whether or not it was ever occupied. Gossip had it, according to Ochelli, that the box was to be for her pet goat—third or fourth offspring from her girlhood pet in Modena—which would invariably enjoy nibbling on the upholstered settee. I suspect the whole thing to be a joke played at the expense of her companion who was thus, if you will excuse the pun, the butt of such cruel humor.

My next step then, was to write to her. This was not to be an easy task. I had to convince her to give up the luxury and comfort of life as a celebrity in Europe and to endure a month-long voyage on the high seas to come to New York, where few understood the language or appreciated the music; where the theater itself was often smaller than a salon in Europe; where the patrons would gawk at the chandeliers or stand on the wooden benches in the pit, hooting and howling like Visigoths riding off with heads at the end of their pikes. I mentioned none of this, of course. I emphasized only the financial rewards. "America is brimful", I wrote. "Of all the nations, her cup, indeed, runneth over. America is the untried, the untested. It awaits only the man or woman of high spirit and lofty imagination to reap the gold from its rocks. America is the earthly paradise, its Adam seeking to turn his untutored ear to the glories of the human voice!"

Under other circumstances I would have been rather ashamed of using such rhetoric, but the right word in the right place—and to the right people—is often the key to success. And in this case it worked, for within six weeks I was to receive a letter from this Madame Pasta.

Meanwhile, I marveled at how quickly the city had forgotten its troubles. Only two years ago it had become a virtual necropolis and now a new infection had settled in—business had become the order of the day. A sense of exhilaration was everywhere. From Tontine's to Wall Street, from the Battery to Trinity Church, the city was alive with its own prospects. I myself was as anxious to get started as I was during those weeks, almost half a century ago, while I was writing my "Figaro". How often would Mozart come dashing in and thrust into my hands the music to accompany my poetic drama! The sheets would emerge, the ink still wet, white hot from the forge of his mind, untempered, unalloyed, in a neat, uncorrected hand! How often would he intersperse little squibs among the notes: "This shall set them standing"; "This bar is worth a few hundred scuderi!"; "We've made our fortunes, my friend."

My own exhilaration deepened as I opened Madame Pasta's letter:

My dear Lorenzo: (note the familiarity, though we had never met!)

Your letter of the thirteenth found me just in time. I had instructed my agents not to accept any more engagements until the latter part of the year, as Georgio and I must seek some peace and quiet from the turbulence of the public adulation so long accorded me during the course of a prolonged and glorious career.

We were, as a matter of fact, giving serious consideration to visiting America where I had hoped to be able to move about without the entire public fuss attendant on my fame. I have been told that America is engaging as a novelty but rather crude from an artistic point of view. But I would like to see things for myself. I may even supply persistent publishers with some provocative material. You must surely be aware of the growing interest among European readers in the workings of your new adopted country. They clamor almost daily for any scrap of news, any tidbit of information which will whet their appetite for sensation.

Be that as it may, I am intrigued by your offer, not so much for the money which, let me say, must be good, but because I shall probably be the only soprano who can truly claim an international reputation

Georgio, who has proven invaluable, must be given all the courtesies and perquisites you would naturally extend to me. He will be making arrangements with you, including the matter of money, which, as I said,

must be good. You will be hearing from him with the
next post.

We are looking forward to a fruitful American
experience.

Redoubtably,
Pasta

Certainly I was pleased, overjoyed at the prospect of a famous
soprano coming to America at my behest, perhaps even to sing
in one of my own operas. And my excitement grew when, by
the following post, another letter came. True to her word, the
final arrangements were to be made by Georgio. Written in a
florid, excruciatingly correct hand, the vowels delicately curved,
the "T's" so punctiliously crossed, his letter declared the terms
under which Madame Pasta deigned to work:

First, she was to be installed in the finest hotel in the city.
Madame would not insist on the best room. She understood,
naturally, that the best room was often occupied by the mayor
or the President and she did not wish to interfere with national
politics. She detested politics. She refused to share a bed, of course
that was out of the question; and the bed must be large enough
to render comfort as well as to suggest her appropriate status.

Second, the room must be decorated with cherubs or their
suitable angelic representatives. Deeply religious, Madame felt
gratitude to God for His gift to her of a voice and the presence
of these "putti" was a constant inspiration to her. Besides,
they were good luck. Additionally, two other rooms would
be provided—one for Georgio, whose quarters must adjoin
Madame's, the other for her maid.

As for food, Madame wished to be thought a good republican.
When in Rome, etc. In honor of her visit to America she would
be delighted to indulge her catholic taste and thus dine on good,
plentiful American fare, as long as it was properly skinned and
well-cooked.

Fourth, and last—but the last shall be first, as we read in the Gospel—Madame would command no less than one third of the gross receipts and the payment, in advance, of $1000 as an appearance fee.

In closing, Georgio commended Madame to the beautiful American people and assured me of his unqualified respect and of his intention to remain forever my most obedient, humble servant. There was, thankfully, no reference to Madame Pasta's goat.

All in all, I suppose I should have been thankful, even gratified, by Madame's reasonableness. Her terms were rigorous, but I have known divas in the Old World who were far less obliging and far greedier. Besides, my passion for bringing Italian opera to America was stronger now than my sense of good business. Within a week I had accepted the terms in writing, setting forth the schedule and the program. We would begin, of course, with my own "Figaro".

I lost no time. Madame would arrive in six weeks and there was much to do. I arranged with Mr. Simpson to reserve the Park Theater. His terms were not as severe as I thought they would be, but I could tell from the expression on his face—the way he contained a smile and the way his eyes took on a bemused glint—that he thought me a fool. I was using my own money, and he knew it.

For the next few weeks I took out frequent notices in *The Daily Advertiser* advising of the arrival of "the great Madame Pasta". Handbills (they cost me $1.75 but I could not scrimp) announced "the magnificent operatic performance by the renowned Madame Pasta." I made it known by word of mouth of the coming of Madame Pasta. Everyone in Riley's spoke of Madame Pasta. At Tontine's men ate their chowder, drank their wine and toasted Madame Pasta. At the Club the members bespoke of Madame Pasta.

All these preparations cost money, but my calculations were honed to the last scruple:

Correspondence to Europe (Ochelli, Pasta et. al.) $1.25

Passage for Pasta &co...$147.50

Pasta's appearance fee $1000.00

Rental of Park Theater (Tues. and Sat. only, sets included) $150.00

Rental of Pasta's rooms at Broadway Hotel

    (including cherubs)..$118.00

All meals (including welcoming dinner for Pasta) $327.50

Orchestra (16 pieces, locally recruited) $188.00

Alterations for costumes (provided by Pasta)........................$9.00

Flowers for Madame's performances and boudoir

(May be saved for three days if kept in willow water) $2.00

Incidental expenses (coaches, daily amusements, etc. $12.00

Total $1955.25

This was by no means a trifling sum, especially since it represented a near-depletion of my savings. There was also the matter of Madame Pasta's seizure of one third of the gate receipts. But I calculated that the cost of the venture would be a pittance compared to the profit to be made. I would get $2.00 for each box seat, $1.50 each in the parquette section and a tidy $1.00 apiece for the benches in the pit. Those standing in the gallery would fetch 75 cents apiece. Subtracting Pasta's one third share from the total would still leave me with a handsome profit.

What a blessing from the gods it is to live one's dream while putting money in one's purse! The great lady arrived—that is to say, the ship carrying her, the *Sir Galahad*, Liverpool—on a rainy October morning. The cranky wind and rain were, ironically, welcomed guests that day, for the weather had been warmer than usual for that time of year, and some people were fearful of the cholera's return. Dr. Francis, in that confident way of his, scoffed at the prospect. But the desperate and the bored seemed pleased that they had something to worry about.

The *Sir Galahad* was moored at Coenti's Slip and I was standing on the dock in the pouring rain, waiting for the great lady's descent. I had hired a coach to escort Madame to her hotel, and the coachman was beginning to grumble at our lady's tardiness as he held the reins, dripping wet.

For a full twenty minutes I waited, my umbrella collapsing in the wind. Madame was nowhere to be seen. There was no sign, no acknowledgment. It was as if the *Sir Galahad* had drifted in with only a thin compliment of a crew, a few of whom I could see scurrying about the rigging, like flies in a web. A couple of the sailors finally came down the gangway, bags over their shoulders. But still no sign of Madame.

After a lengthy stand in the rain I lost patience and feared something amiss.

I made my way up the gangway, bumping into a couple of sailors coming down, and on reaching the deck asked one of the crew for Madame Pasta's cabin. He pointed to a door leading below and I took the steps, carefully you may be sure, into a small corridor dimly lit and rank with the odors of humanity confined for some three thousand miles at sea.

Her cabin was at the end of the corridor and I knocked on the door. Instantly I heard a scuffle, as if someone were moving heavy furniture. There was a muffled expostulation, an exclamation of shock or surprise, and then silence, as if whoever was behind the door was holding his breath in hopes of my going away.

But I did not go away. I must have stood by that door for a full minute before knocking again. This time the door opened. Standing before me was the oddest creature I had ever seen. He was smaller than my walking stick, standing only to the height of my waist. His legs were bowed and one leg was shorter than the other so that he tilted slightly to one side, as if he were standing on an incline. His large head appeared to sit squarely on his shoulders without the aid of a neck. It simply squatted there like a melon.

It was surmounted by a blue turban, swathed about his ears like a muff. He was dressed in an exquisite silk robe that was fitted perfectly to his body. He wore no shoes and his feet were covered with hose but hastily installed. He was obviously winded, as if from great exertion, but tried to disguise his laborious breathing by keeping his lips taut and puffing through his nose.

He looked at me impatiently, tilting his head. For an instant I imagined it rolling off the edge of his shoulder, as from a table.

"And you are . . ." he asked, as if annoyed.

"I am Signor Lorenzo Da Ponte, here to greet Madame Pasta."

"Aaaahh!" he moaned, suddenly aggrieved. He swiveled about violently, waving his hand as if to say "come in, come in", and betook himself to a corner of the room where an open trunk brimmed over with pillows. Into this he climbed, hitching up his robe. I could see his bare legs that in the half-light gave off a waxy sheen, like the rind of an uncured cheese.

He made himself comfortable amid the pillows and when he had settled in he began shaking his head, clicking his tongue in disapproval. In his blue turban and robe, his feet dangling, he evoked the image of a Turk embowered in a miniature harem.

"Madame is disturbed, sir," he said. "Very disturbed. You have violated our trust."

Before I had a chance even to consider these words a voice called out from the shadows. Here let me note that the cabin, despite its little window opposite the door, was a cramped, fetid habitat, no larger than a cell in a Venetian prison. I was surprised, then, almost shocked, to hear another voice, for its owner would have no place to hide, and my first impression was that the figure in the trunk was the cabin's only occupant. But soon I discerned, just beyond the trunk, vaguely outlined in the gloom, a large screen. Behind it, I could make out a makeshift bunk, the rumpled bedclothes tousled into hills and valleys.

"I can speak for myself, Georgio," the voice said. "Signor Da Ponte, I am disturbed. Very disturbed. You have violated our trust."

A large woman emerged from behind the screen, gathering herself into an ample dressing gown. She too gave the impression of answering a summons in great haste. As she approached she put her hand on Georgio's shoulder, as if to soothe him, as a mistress her unruly hound.

So this was Madame Pasta who was to be the keystone to my arching success.

As she stood with her back to the window I realized at once that Ochelli was right.

Not fat and not young, she loomed like some imposing contradiction. I could not tell, for instance, how much of the figure she showed was her own; how much of it was covered by her dressing gown, ample enough as it was to embrace even Georgio amid its tufted folds. Her figure gave off an aura of sturdy sensuality, but there was something in her presence that suggested only a tentative grasp of the wholesome. She was, as Ochelli had warned, simply on the verge. One got the distinct impression that her life had moved along a series of innumerable verges, this being only the latest, if not the last. Withal, she seemed consciously disciplined, as if only desperately holding on to a willful self-control, fortified by an experience dearly bought and paid for. Like Georgio, she was wearing a turban, but hers was not fitted. It seemed hastily slipped over her head, and she too breathed heavily in controlled puffs.

"I am very much disturbed," she repeated.

"What is it?" I said. "I was beginning to think something was wrong."

"Something *is* wrong," said Georgio. "Terribly wrong."

"Something *is* wrong," Madame echoed. "Terribly wrong."

"You never mentioned," she went on, "that the city is unsafe."

"Unsafe?"

"Georgio and I were perfectly willing to live up to the terms of our contract, but that's all over now."

"My dear Madame Pasta, what is the trouble? What do you mean?"

She placed her hands on her hips, like a woman about to confront the laundry tub.

"No one is leaving this ship. We're not going ashore. If it were not for the pilot who came aboard last night and happened to mention it to the captain who in turn happened to mention it to Georgio, we would have been unmercifully exposed. We would both be dead. Our tongues will dry up."

"Madame is talking cholera, you scoundrel," said Georgio from the trunk. "You failed to advise us of the unhealthy situation here. Contract, indeed! Madame is thinking of suing. Isn't that right, Madame?"

"I'm thinking of suing," said Madame.

I was beginning to see a boiling pot. I have not lived more than three score and ten years without knowing when the world is practicing perfidy. It was obvious now that Madame had conned her part from Georgio. Together they were going to rob me, and I sensed that I had little chance of preventing them. Nevertheless, I must try to cover my own desperation:

"I'm sure Madame has misunderstood," I said. "The cholera is long gone. I don't know what the pilot could have told you. There was certainly no need of my mentioning anything like that in my letters, as the cholera is a thing of the past and therefore irrelevant,"

"Do you call Madame's exposure to death irrelevant?" said Georgio. "I call it thoughtless and deceitful."

"It *is* deceitful," said Madame. "I had been under the impression that America was fresh and wild and naturally immune from the ills and plagues of Europe. You cannot pay me enough, Signor Da Ponte. No! I cannot, I shall not, I dare not risk my life!"

Here she beat her clenched fist into her open palm. And when she turned to Georgio for verification, I knew at once that both had, indeed, sprung a trap, and that Madame was playing a role more nefarious than any she had ever played on the stage. It seemed sensible now to remonstrate with Georgio as the chief conspirator.

"Look here," I said. "Let us not talk of suing, for we both know that only the lawyers will profit. We will find ourselves bereft of any fortunes we could make here. You must certainly know that the cholera is gone. *I* have not the cholera. No one in New York has the cholera. If you go back to Europe you will have made a long voyage for nothing. You will lose a great deal of money, and the opportunity of furthering Madame's career, to say nothing of your own."

This last remark was calculated to irritate Georgio. I was sure he would be insulted by the imputation against his character as Madame's quartermaster. But to my surprise he suddenly sprang from the trunk, as if he had been sitting on a hot stove. Putting his hands together as if in prayer, he tilted his head once again and closed his eyes.

"What you say has some truth. Perhaps it is not you who are the scoundrel, but that wretched pilot. There was something I didn't trust about him from the beginning. But I am here to protect Madame."

(Here I heard Madame Pasta sigh, and look at Georgio forlornly.)

"She must not be subjected to any kind of peril. This American engagement was to have been only partly business. Madame wishes to travel. She wishes to see the great Niagara, perhaps a tamed Indian or two. She does not expect to have her tongue dry up. Whether there is cholera or not, whether you mentioned it or not, Madame must be satisfied. She must not be jeopardized."

By this time Madame Pasta had taken a chair by the trunk. Putting her head back, she closed her eyes and put her fist to her forehead. "Oh, I can feel the poison in the very air I breathe," she gasped. "My body throbs with every lap of the sea beneath me. The very boards I trod groan with impending death!"

The whole thing was out now.

"So. You mean to hold me up, like common bandits," I told Georgio. I was not afraid of him. His cupidity had spared him the pretense of moral outrage.

"Bandits?' he said. His hands were still folded as in prayer, but now they were brought close to his lips, as if he were kissing his fingers. "This is not an opera, my friend. This is business. This is saving Madame Pasta!"

"We should sail immediately," said Madame Pasta, apparently unaware that the crew had left the ship. "I can almost feel my tongue drying up."

I realized, of course, that I would have to give in. Most of my cash and all of my honor had gone into this venture and it was too late now to make other arrangements. Georgio must have realized it, too, for he stood his little ground with all the smug detachment of a paid executioner. As much as I wanted to smash the little toad with my stick, as much as it would have done my heart good to stuff the creature into that trunk of his, I knew that to do so would ruin my hopes of bringing Italian opera to America. Years of commercial struggles had come to this. My second destiny was held hostage to thieves. Things were not different in America, after all. The same caution, the same need for adaptability, ruled here with the equal force it did in the courts of Vienna or in the salons of Venice. A man must need to show deference as a matter of politics but maintain his dignity as the mark of his self-respect. I may bow to the Emperor, but I will not kneel.

I was not in the presence of the Emperor now, but the need to temporize, to keep my self-respect, was nonetheless vital. I would not rant; even less would I beg. I knew that Georgio was a thief, and he knew that I knew. My best chance then was to play his game, to keep up the illusion which both of us recognized as no longer necessary. In this way, at least, I would be able to salvage something for myself. I could not count on Georgio's generosity, but I could rely on his vanity. I could invite him to filch my watch, in hopes of his leaving me the chain.

"Madame must be brave," I began. "There is only danger for the faint of heart. How much, then, does Madame require to exercise her bravery? How much more must we pay for her to risk death?"

Georgio opened his eyes, smiled and turned to Madame Pasta, still in the thralldom of her pestilential fear. I could see him mentally calculating. He hopped over to his trunk and seated himself amid the pillows, as if on a throne from which he issued his *ex cathedra* pronouncements.

"Madame would risk it, would be willing to sacrifice a moiety of safety in the interests of her art for . . . let us say, two-thirds of the take."

I stared in outraged disbelief.

"That is the price for Madame's bravery."

"I'm not leaving the ship," said Madame. "We should sail immediately!"

I knew that I would be ruined. Even if the venture succeeded—as I knew it would—my share would be so little as to make the enterprise no more profitable to me than if I had hired myself out as a day laborer for the new Erie canal. As a man, I would find some way to get even. My honor, not to mention the condition of my poor pocketbook, demanded that I seek all means to exact an appropriate vengeance on this basilisk, this viper. I would find a way to pay them back. For now, I kept quiet. I would have to accept their terms. Still, Italian Opera would have come to America, to New York! And I, Lorenzo Da Ponte, was to be the instrument of its begetting.

*   *   *

FOURTEEN

The Tourist

American Notions: Native Views from Foreign Eyes
—Observations and opinions of a famous diva
on the manners and morals of the Americans
by her faithful friend
and companion
Lady Georgina I.M. Small

Chapter the First
On the denizens of New York

I have been milady's travelling companion long enough to appreciate deeply her amiable disposition and the uncommon breadth of her genius. She has sung in all the great opera houses of Europe, has performed by special invitation of royal princes and men of princely means, and has dazzled all the world with her grace, her charm and the beauty of her magnificent voice. All the world, that is, except America. To this cultural hinterland, this erstwhile howling wilderness inhabited only by savage bears and bare savages, her beauteous form and sacred pipes had never been seen or heard. Never had they—as in Europe—transformed the very landscape with their sublime force; never had they exercised their power to "charm insensate rocks and running streams" (Ovid, translated by Lady Georgina I.M. Small).

It was this lacuna in her career that prompted milady's decision—half in the interests of charity, half in pure adventurousness—to voyage to America.

Thus it was that one late September morning we boarded a packet from Liverpool, Captain Amos Grunge, bound for New York. For the first time in milady's life, she felt the harsh swells of the Atlantic heave beneath her angelic bosom. Every barbarous wave sent a thrilling rush into her very being, piercing, jabbing, penetrating to the vital core of her soul, searing her innards with the white hot twisting thrust, borne up by the exhilaration and fear naturally begotten by a long journey at sea.

The voyage began innocently enough. Only two days out, the weather bracing, the air clean, the sky clear as glass. On fine days such as these we lunched with Captain Grunge by the poop. The mizzenmast topsail snapped to like a singing wire. Life in the foc'sle was merry and gay. The mainsail had been braced and we were tacking smartly.

But five days out the wind shifted and the sky turned the color of slate. The very air pricked; the sea snarled. A storm was brewing, a howling Nor'Easter, and the ship was all astir. Below decks all portables had to be stowed, spliced, belayed and battened down. The storm jibs were made to. Grunge ordered the staysails between the masts to be fastened and the flying jib boom secured. But a huge swell threw us all off course. The topsail halyards let go and we were close-hauled upon the wind, the ship almost lying over on her beam end. The quick-thinking mate, a Mr. Spaniel, sprang to and saved the ship from broaching, though as she came up the studding sail boom gave way, the clew lined buckled and another fierce yaw and a come-to snapped the guys. To Grunge's horror, the outhaul block gave way and the halyard splices split, the sail blowing round the spitsail yard and the head guys. To make the situation worse, the starboard studding sails, outrigged on her foremast, had to be brought in.

Even now I tremble at the thought of that horrid storm. Only he who has never been to sea would gloss over such an experience; only he who has ne'er felt his timbers shiver in the ferocity of wind and rain; in short, only he who has no soul, would pass on without so much as even a sigh. I swear to you, dear reader, milady almost died. For two whole nights I stayed by her bed, keeping vigil over her troubled frame. Her glorious bosom heaved steadily in an uneasy sleep and I sensed the inquietude of her dreams—the hot, piercing, twisting, throbbing succubus that lay upon her, the night-rider from Hell, the fiend nightmare come galloping, penetrating the very private parts of milady's delicious slumbers.

Within a day or two, however, she recovered. Under my most solicitous attention she took nourishment and soon regained sufficient strength to go on deck, there to breathe in the sea air which, on the morning of October 19, brought with it the tinge of sweetness that only the certitude of land could hold. Sure enough, we heard the lookout cry "Land-ho!" and peering over the taffrail we got our first glimpse of the New World.

Contrary to our expectations, there was no wilderness to be seen. The only forests, to be sure, had become transformed into a vast thicket of spars, bowsprits and a maze of tall-masted ships riding at anchor at the edge of a narrow island that sat at the head of a wide, deep bay. This was New York. Not a particularly large place; there was nothing unusual about it. It looked for all the world like a village that had gotten away from itself. Except for an atmosphere of thick commerce that could be almost *felt*, New York could easily be dismissed as a farm boy's version of London or Paris. Its primary appeal, as I have tried to suggest, was its aura of energy, its tonic enthusiasm, as easily inhaled as its fresh, healthful air.

Yet, energy alone would not redeem the place from its crassness, its mad pursuit of mercantile interests. But this in another chapter!

It was a rainy, chilly day. Milady and I had already been preparing to leave the ship when we were greeted at the gangplank by none other than the Mayor himself! His honor had come aboard, as he proclaimed, to greet milady and personally escort her to her hotel where suitable arrangements had already been made. Needless to say, Madam Pasta—(Ah, the name is out, so let it be!) Madam Pasta, I say, was embarrassed. She had been hoping to arrive *incognito*, as it were, to see for herself, in the person of a private, ordinary low citizen, life at first hand in this new republic of America. But her fame had sailed ahead, it seems, and her *incognito*-ness had leaked out. Such is the price of notoriety!

The Mayor was an elderly man, about 70, simply dressed. Well-worn but well-tended, his clothing certainly typified that quality of *commonality* about which Americans are always fond of braying. But we cannot help asking whether *commonality*—suggesting homage to the basic dignity of all men—is really a form of *mediocrity,* a tribute rather to the vulgarity of the herd, a vulgarity so pervasive in American life, in dress as well as in manner.

His honor carried a wondrous walking stick, to which he seemed supremely tender, carrying it under his arm, as if shielding it from the weather. The headpiece was remarkably worked in gold, but I could not make out its details.

His honor bowed as he introduced himself—I will not divulge his name in the interests of journalistic integrity; I eschew libel and controversy)—and then expressed the hope that milady would sanctify the city with her singing, perhaps in a series of performances. Madame thanked his honor, but reminded him of her wish to be an anonymous traveler and of her aim to learn openly about the little people of this land. The Mayor, however, ignored her plea. So forcefully did he persist and cajole that in the end milady came to the disturbing conclusion that she would not be permitted to set foot in America—or in New York, at any rate, unless she acceded to his remonstrances, or should I say THREATS.

Here let it be said that the Mayor was not a bad man. Indeed, there was an air of dignity and a secure sense of worldliness about him. He was a man who seemed quite used to the art of compromise, at ease in the practice of a kind of tactful civility. But his importunities were a transparent sign that, like most Americans, he had come to regard art as a commodity, something bought and traded for, as if it were a species of beaver hat or a rare whalebone stay.

As if to prove my point, the Mayor here reached into his coat pocket and pulled out a contract, the terms already drawn and the terms specified. They were, to be sure, niggardly enough. Milady's matchless genius was to be purchased at the cost of her captivity. She was to receive the city's hospitality but only a staple fee, as if she were a hired hand. To mollify, his honor vowed to serve as her personal guide, escorting her among the city's shrines and temples and holy places.

By the time we left the ship, expressing our fond farewells and heartfelt gratitude to Captain Grunge, the rain had let up and the sky was clearing. His honor had arranged to send ahead our luggage in a cart, so the three of us climbed into a waiting coach and made our way to the hotel.

At first we expected to proceed up Broadway, but the Mayor, as if struck by a thought, quickly directed the driver to turn off and go on by a shorter route to our destination. Madame had barely made herself comfortable when we were violently unsettled by the ragged motion of the coach. To our horror we discerned that the unpaved roads in New York were no better than irrigation ditches. The rain had softened even this well-worn path. Ruts gouged out from the ceaseless runs of wagons and carts sliced across the road. Puddles abounded, rills and holes greeted the coach at every revolution of its muddied wheels. At one spot our coach bogged down in a slough of mud.

His honor seemed embarrassed, genuinely concerned. He suggested that, since the hotel was but a stone's throw away, it would be more convenient to debark and proceed on foot to her rooms, where she would be regaled with a hearty American breakfast and a warm bath. Wishing to be a democrat on this occasion—when in Rome, etc.—milady accepted the Mayor's proposal and began what was to be a short, uneventful perambulation to the hotel. But the stone's throw distance for Americans was indeed a cannon ball's flight for the rest of mankind, for after what seemed an interminable slog through the mud, during which milady and I both nearly sank midway down our limbs, we were told by his honor that the place was but "another block or two".

But now the horror! As milady made her way up Broadway Road, modestly walking merely, not gazing or talking, a monstrous great hog came grunting from behind and nuzzling at her ankles with its hairy snout, sent milady tumbling into the mud. The vicious porker thereupon thrust his filthy snout amid milady's flounces and furbelows, snorting with eager exhalations, as if her petticoats were the lairs of some priceless truffles.

Once again, his honor seemed solicitous, but I reckoned that there was an odd, almost amused glint in his eye. Surely he must have known of the possibility of such a froward (sic.) occurrence, for vicious swine and crazed bovines ceaselessly roam this thoroughfare from morning till night. The reader will have little difficulty imagining milady's profound shock and mortal detestation. To have come three thousand miles amid stormy seas and foul winds only to be attacked by some wretched farmer's marauding porker was an abuse of milady's person unparalleled in a life and career otherwise filled only with glory. Now she was covered with filth. His honor, let me repeat, seemed almost too zealous, too solicitous, too eager to ameliorate milady's condition. She, for her part, lay in the ditch scarcely breathing, and it was only with the greatest effort of his honor and the coachman who had run up to help that we managed to get her to the so-called hotel.

I will not pause here to describe the place, though I am fully aware that travel writers owe their readers the satisfaction of a justified curiosity. But I was so unnerved by the morning's events that I cannot in good conscience accurately recall my first impressions of the hotel. Let me say only that it *seemed* satisfactory at first, though in the garish light of such an untoward adventure one could not fully appreciate its rustic charm without harboring the fear that at any moment another giant pig might come snorting into the lobby and scramble wildly up the stairs.

After the exertions of such an arrival, Madame thought it best to remain in her room, there to indulge in the luxury of a bath and in the recuperative powers of a nap. His honor, too, had urged that she rest, assuring her that all arrangements would be taken care of. Meanwhile, he said, he would find the owner of the pig and exact restitution. What precisely he would do, I could not say, but there was a renewed energy in his walk as he left us. His flight down the stairs was borne with the vigor of a man intent on carrying out a grand design.

The next day his honor sent word that he would call on us late in the afternoon. He said in his note that, as a kind of peace offering for yesterday's offense against milady's dignity—to say nothing of my own—he had arranged an outing to Bloomingdale, one of the city's more elegant private estates. There, he assured us, we would be entertained in a style more befitting milady's station.

Meanwhile we were to breakfast, not at the hotel, but at a place called Tontine's. A coach took us there—near a place they call the Battery—and we were escorted into a private room looking out upon a wide verandah and the tumult of the city beyond. But more of that anon.

It strikes me as appropriate in this place to make some brief observations on the peculiarities of an American breakfast. They eat no fruit—the Americans, I mean—except for a local variety of grape which, to a refined palate like Madame's, has what I could only describe as a wild, wolfish taste, sweet but somehow unrefreshing. Meat is everywhere in their diet. They consume more venison, more lamb, more beef and most of all, more pork than any three nations in Europe. The Americans are particularly fond of pork. It is as ubiquitous as the runnels in their roads. As milady and I sat at our breakfast, we could only marvel at the multitude of ways and means their culinary wits could devise in the preparation of pork. It is diced and served in a kind of pie or dumpling; it is finely chopped and served as a kind of thick chip; it is cut into strips called bacon; it is served as a steak, a chop, even a sauce; it is dried, soaked, salted; it is baked, fried, broiled, breaded and boiled; it is even presented in a kind of soup. For myself I could not help thinking of his honor's assurance the day before that he would seek redress on that porker and its owner. More than once during the meal I imagined I was looking down into my plate at the remains of that porcine beastie that tried to feast on milady's ankles.

They also serve a kind of yellow sweet roll which they call a muffin and is made largely from milled corn The bread is very good—hearty and rich. As for liquid refreshment, milady insisted on only their best champagne. The waiter recommended an American brew, an imitation concocted from some vegetable mixed with brandy and honey. But with the memory of the porker still green, milady preferred the European and in the end we ordered a bottle of Bever Sillery Baun, very dry, at two dollars, fifty, charged, of course, to his honor.

After breakfast we strolled along the verandah until the cacophony of shouts, the stomping of pedestrians and the clanging of cargo generated such a pandemonium that milady felt a headache coming on and returned to her room for rest and to await the Mayor.

As promised, he arrived about one in the afternoon. He greeted us in his usual way—in that odd mixture of formal politeness and informal cordiality, as one king, for example, would greet another. He had suited himself in new apparel, a spanking bright beaver hat topping off a gray coat and shiny green cravat. Even his walking stick, to which, as I have said, he seemed almost reverentially tender, even this had been polished in honor of the excursion.

"I'm sure Madame Pasta will enjoy this treat," he said, getting into the coach. As we proceeded, his honor grew increasingly excited. He became almost too extravagant in his praise, calling Bloomingdale "a noble pile, commanding an even nobler prospect", situated about eight miles north in a section called Morningside Heights. Even more extravagant was his depiction of "the magnificent hospitality" of Mrs. Buell, mistress of the estate. "A most learned woman, a most exquisite hostess, a most matchless companion," he exclaimed, looking pointedly at me.

I would have been prepared to take the mayor at his word except for two extenuations. For one, his honor seemed too unrestrained in his praise. For another, our adventure with the swine had already hardened my distrust of the local institutions and had stiffened my cynicism about the diurnal ministrations of American life. Not to be too fine: any city likely to put its people at risk by the casual depredations of marauding livestock must be suspect as a civic vessel of elegance and refinement.

Be that as it may, we certainly enjoyed the ride, as Broadway veered toward the broad expanse of the North river and then narrowed to a country lane, lined on both sides by stately trees which the people here call American elms.

His honor sat opposite us, his walking stick propped in front of him, his hands clasped on its head. After a while he ceased his encomia about Bloomingdale and Mrs. Buell, enjoying instead the passing scene in silence, a trace of a smile on his face, as if remembering a pleasant moment in his life.

An hour's jaunt brought us within the precincts of the estate. In spite of initial misgivings, I found myself impressed by the place as our coach rolled to a halt just outside the gates.

The large red brick building with its stained-glass windows stood on a rise a few hundred paces beyond. Behind it we could see the North river narrowing itself among the trees. The neatly trimmed grounds were defined by a high iron fence running along the perimeter and down to the water's edge. I have visited many estates in Europe, particularly in England where the owners were extraordinarily uxorious about their lands, as wary of them, indeed, as a new husband his wife. But for all that, their estates never were enclosed. Here, however, the iron fence with its spear-like tips shouted rudely at us, giving notice not so much of established property rights, as of a kind of remorseless discourtesy.

His honor asked us to remain in the coach while he went within to inform the mistress of our arrival. When he did not return—we thought it odd that he should have needed personally to announce us in the first place—we were beginning to grow concerned at his absence. Suddenly the front door opened and a man in a brown apron appeared. Standing there in the doorway he struck a most contradictory note. Could he be a worker, a member of the household, even a mechanic of some sort? Was he involved in some capacity with the stables or with one of the outbuildings, two of which we could see down near the water? If so, what was he doing at the front door, acting for all the world like a butler or, God help us, the master himself? We understood that Americans prided themselves on an almost ferocious commitment to democratic behavior, perhaps even to the point of communing with their servants. Kings and emperors were no better at an American's table than a shopkeeper or the proprietor of an inn. And this fellow, even as he made his way to our coach, acted for all the world like the proprietor of the place, though, as we were soon to learn, he was no more than a king in his own small domain.

"Mrs. Buell is expecting you," he said, holding open the door and extending an arm to milady as she descended. As we followed him up the walk and into the house, the man in the brown apron assured us that his honor was already inside, attending to some unexpected business with friends.

As stately as the house was from without, there was an odd, Spartan sparseness about it from within. The white plaster walls were pocked as if by a ceaseless barrage of musket balls and the high ceilings and porticoed hall presented an unexpectedly jarring elegance amid the ugly chairs and wooden benches set uninvitingly against the walls. We felt no comfort, no sense of hospitality here. A whir, as of some distant and incessant motion, dinned in our ears. For one moment we thought we heard a shout, a human-like bark, and then a clatter, as of wood on wood. In another room to our left someone was speaking, but we could not hear clearly what was being said. From somewhere deep in the house a man laughed. Above us, a tattoo of feet thrummed along the floor.

Our anxiety was increasing, especially since the Mayor was still not to be seen and the man in the brown apron, who only a few minutes ago acted like the proprietor, now simply stood mute beside us, as if waiting for something, anything, to sever the pall of strangeness that had descended on us all.

Relief came in the form of a most charming woman who appeared almost miraculously from behind one of the columns. She was tall, graceful, elegant, but though she smiled broadly as she approached, her eyes seemed to be looking beyond us, her gaze fixed on some nameless presence.

"Ah, Mrs. Buell," said the man in the brown apron. "Your guests have arrived."

Mrs. Buell bent her body in an exaggerated bow, swooping from the waist, her arm extended in greeting. She reminded me of a marionette suddenly bereft of its strings. I could not venture a guess as to her age, but her green dress, stylish when new, was of another time. We were shocked, milady and I, to observe that it was none too clean. Like her dress, her coif had not been in fashion since the French Revolution. Her hair rose in abundant curls and braided rings, and, most astonishingly, was surmounted by an iron key which, suspended by a pink ribbon, dangled off the top of her head. It was an old heavy key, and nudged her temple when she moved.

Milady and I looked at each other. If this were a style keenly favored by the new American "beau monde", it was one, indeed, that we were prepared to ignore. Opportunities for adopting such a fashion abounded back at the hotel, where any of a dozen keys could easily be had.

"How good of you to come," said Mrs. Buell. "I'm sure you must be tired after such a long journey. Allow me to offer you some refreshment. Sambo, bring my people into the parlor."

Sambo—a most peculiar name for our white man in the brown apron—smiled crookedly and escorted us down the porticoed hall. As we walked we could see a large, brightly lit room at the end and assumed it to be our destination. But suddenly we were mortified, flabbergasted, shocked, astounded—call it what you will—words fail me. Walking out of that room and approaching us was a short, bald man about fifty, whose wrinkled, hairy paunch was made all the more disgusting by the fact that he was stark naked. Onward he came, his feet and his shins filthy. He shuffled along like a sleepwalker, his eyes open, taking no notice of us.

When he reached a few paces from us—milady and I had naturally froze—he abruptly stopped, fell back against the wall and slid to the floor, bringing his knees under his chin. Then he raised one hand and with an open palm covered his left eye.

With his free eye he perused his other hand, noticed his thumb, then stuck it into his mouth and began sucking on it.

For a while we could not move, but Sambo, or whatever his name was, quickly grabbed milady's arm and carried us away. We were brought not to the brightly-lit room—indeed we dreaded it now—but to a door just off the hall, to a room where Mrs. Buell was already waiting for us.

This was not a parlor, but something like a bedroom, except that it resembled a barrack or a monk's retreat. The lone window opposite the door was but recently gouged out, its iron bars interrupting a view of a distant little stream choked with stones and the roots of dead trees. The room itself contained a small wall mirror, a bare, wooden-plank table with four chairs and, against a wall, an unmade bed, a worn blanket rumpled at its foot. On top of the table was a cracked teapot with no tray beneath it. Four un-matching china cups, chipped and without handles were arranged around the pot, and Mrs. Buell, wiping her hands down the sides of her dress, bid us be seated.

At this point milady and I thought it best to follow through with the adventure. To put the most favorable construction on the episode and do justice to our hostess, we could assume that Mrs. Buell was living now mostly on her reputation. Perhaps, we thought, she was once rich, but—like many we had known in Europe—had now only her land upon which to subsist. Financial reverses, even in America, had left her as we saw her, in such straightened circumstances. As for the naked man, he, indeed, could easily be explained—or so we would have liked to believe. He was a relation, perhaps her own husband, whose mind had broken by the reverses of the family situation. Indeed, milady and I have known a number of wealthy friends in Europe whose intellects had become unhinged by the collapse of several banks during Napoleon's time.

Meanwhile we were at a loss to find his honor. Where *had* the Mayor gone? Why was he leaving us alone, without even so much as an "excuse me"? And what was the nature of his business that he should so insultingly ignore his guests?

"What a pleasure it is to have guests," said Mrs. Buell. Reaching for the teapot, she smiled and began to pour, but whether we preferred tea, or coffee, or any other beverage, made little practical difference. Though she held each of our cups under the spout; though she tilted the pot so elegantly, her little finger poised like a question mark; though she inclined he head amiably, as if watching the brew flow deliciously into our cups; though for all the world she behaved like the perfect hostess, we were never to satisfy our taste. For the pot was empty, and as the philosophers declare, "Nothing comes from nothing."

When she was done pouring air into our cups she sat next to milady. Madame, to be sure, was inclined to move her chair away from Mrs. Buell but thought better of her intention when she noticed Sambo shaking his head and pursing his lips, as if to say "no!"

"You know," she said. "The birds are such mean cargo, aren't they? Butterflies are much more accommodating, although, of course, for a real treat I think scallions make for a wonderful swim. Sambo, where are the cakes? There are no cakes. Where are the cakes, Sambo?"

The brown-aproned fellow merely smiled and shrugged.

Mrs. Buell sipped her air. Then she put down her cup, folding one hand on the other.

"Of course," she continued. "Rainbows have elegance beyond the bitterness of bolted doors. Do bear in mind that the true cabbage has no warts, except, of course, when it is in flight. They tell me it's going to rain tomorrow. Do you think we ought to bathe in our coffins? I have a needle that will fill the hole that Uncle Grandpa carved out of a piece of licorice. Oh, I am so delighted to see you. I've written a special song, just for the occasion. Would you like to hear it?"

"We should be delighted," interposed our man in the brown apron. He looked at us and shook his head, putting his finger to his lips.

Mrs. Buell reached up and started to twirl the key around her hair with her fingers as she sang:

"My thwarted love, just like the dove
That at the dawn 'gins flying
Sits on the tree, O, woe is me,
While I, poor chick, be dying
Tra-la, Tee-hee, Ho-ho
While I, poor chick, be dying.

As on the morn a babe is born,
Into the world comes crying,
So too my fate—too short, too late—
Exhausts itself in sighing.
Tra-la, Tee-hee, Ho-ho.
Exhausts itself in sighing.

Ta rum, ta rum ta rum.

"How wonderful!" I exclaimed, not only to forestall our friend in the apron but to humor Mrs. Buell as well, for if the truth be told, I was beginning to grow fearful of our lives. Such fear, however, was itself short-lived, for even as Mrs. Buell had finished singing, her eyes took on a distant gaze and she fell silent.

This was the moment we had been waiting for, and we did not linger. Quickly, Sambo motioned for us to get up, which we did, and in the next moment we were making our way out of the room, up the porticoed hall and out of the house, still to the sounds of laughter and clattering and an odd thump on the upper floor.

The Mayor would certainly have some heavy explaining to do. We vowed to confront him, that rascal, as soon as we got back to the hotel.

*   *   *

FIFTEEN

The Reviewer
How Da Ponte's investment fared

Madame Pasta sang last night and all New York took note. Gentlemen removed their hats; the ladies sighed and swooned. Even the customary hooting Goths standing on the wooden benches of the pit—now refurbished for this occasion with blue upholstered chairs, minus, of course, the antimacassars—even they sat silently, suborning their brutish sensibilities to the charms of Madame's dulcet tones. Indeed, before last night New Yorkers had never heard such melodious liquefaction and thus were appropriately spellbound. Certainly even the most equable of us needed to be. How else were we to put up with the impertinent bustling of a grotesque little man who snapped directions about the four quarters of the playhouse and insisted on supervising every aspect of the production, from ticket sales to the amount of illumination suffusing the stage?

Our sources inform us that this impudent gnome had been observed literally counting the empty seats in advance of the performance and making notations in his little brown book. He was even spotted with Da Ponte in the gallery, the two of them outlining in chalk exact spots for the spectators to stand, so many inches of space for each. In the boxes, he moved the settees farther to the rear and had more chairs brought in.

He gave orders as to the scrim behind the stage, inquired as to the number of musicians in the orchestra, and their salaries, and scowled at what he called the "crepuscular illumination" which fell on Madame's shoulders as she sang. During the performance, this reviewer watched the fellow counting the glasses in the bar, imbibing copiously, by the by, both the champagne and the brandy, for the purpose of assessing, in his words, "the quality of the refreshments."

Rumor has it that there is bad blood between this little man and Mr. Da Ponte, perhaps even involving Madame herself. What the nature of this quarrel is we do not pretend to know. A few wags have unkindly suggested that the feud is as old and as unseemly as that involving Achilles and his prized Briseis. But they are impudent wags and we are not here to besmirch anybody's name. Suffice it to say that whatever ill will existed among the parties has been put to bed—excuse the shameless and unintended pun—in the interest of Art and the business of Art.

Even if this little man is, as we have been told, Madame Pasta's agent and general factotum, we will make no invidious remarks against him. Our place is not to stand in judgment of Madame's taste or discretion. We are here—if we may invert the Bard—rather not to bury Caesar but to praise him. Indeed, Madame Pasta's voice must stand as the lodestone of all earthly encomiums. It can achieve a bottom A and proceed to a high C# or even D. Her portimento was particularly fine and her gift for ornamentation admirable. Her recitative was passionate, yet subdued; rational, yet frenzied. Her legato was remarkably liquid and soothing, while she sustained a vibrato of unsurpassed delicacy. We are quick to note, however, that she sang the notes of her opening aria a full quarter of a tone too flat, although we must insist that the final song in the ensemble, with its roulades and its scales of shakes ascending to a semitone gave proof through the night that our Pasta was still there.

What we are getting at, frankly, is that the voice made up for a number of shortcomings in her physical appearance. Dressed in purple silk embroidered with green gewgaws, Madame seemed somewhat plodding on the boards. Her arms were fine but her figure lacked softness. There was, to be blunt, more potato and less pate in Madame's gesticulations. As for the role of the Countess Rosina which Madame has taken on—for we forgot to mention that the opera, indeed, was Mr. Da Ponte's own "Marriage of Figaro"—and we purposely use the English (more about that anon)—as for the role of the Countess, as we said, Madame Pasta gave a brave performance. Realizing, no doubt, that she was long past the age which would have made the role of Susanna believable, she rendered the heart-wounded Countess with just the right amount of mature fire, although her vindictiveness towards the Count, particularly in the final scene, was almost too violent for us to bear. One would not have expected such forceful grappling from one with such a voice.

But the voice; ah, the voice! It breathed responsiveness; it seduced the faculties; it intoxicated the soul with its sweetness, quelling the propensity to evil thoughts and evil wishes that all men are heir to. It made us all forget, at least for the moment, the frustration of being unable to understand more than a few words of the story. Despite our convictions of the beauty of the Italian language, despite even Mr. Da Ponte's expostulations in support of "opera's mother-tongue", we nevertheless found ourselves fidgeting in our seats even amid Madame Pasta's soaring vocalics.

Indeed, it is a sublime kind of irritation, but an irritation nonetheless when an obvious joke is being played on stage and peals of laughter come only from a few *cognoscenti* in the boxes. Gentlemen in top hats may smile, and proper ladies titter behind their fans, but we are of the opinion that opera will never be popular in this country so long as it is sung in a tongue nobody can cotton to. Mr. Da Ponte—to whom, by the way, we owe a debt of gratitude for bringing Madame Pasta here and for setting up the "whole shebang"—Mr. Da Ponte may be the only one who appreciates the nuances of the music, but a good story is a good story, "what I say", and that is what the public wants. Gentlemen may cry "Bravo", but give me librettos or give me death! True, Mr. Da Ponte had translated the opera, especially for this occasion. He could be seen sitting at a table in the lobby before the performance and during the intermission, a pile of hastily printed librettos before him. He was selling them for 121/2 cents each, a steep price but one that had to be paid if you were to make any sense at all out of the thing.

And speaking of gentlemen. We are pleased to note the presence in the boxes of some of the city's most illustrious! The mayor was there, of course. Mr. Hone is to be seen only at the best events, and his attendance there will christen the occasion as the most important of the season. His honor, by the way, shares our view that for opera to succeed here, it must be in English.

Also present was Mr. Clement Moore and his sister, Miss Agnes, who, we understand, are personal friends of Mr. Da Ponte. They were sharing a box with the well—known physician, John Francis. It was Dr. Francis, as we all remember, who exerted great heroism during the late epidemic. We have it on good authority that Dr. Francis speaks tolerable Italian, or at least understands as much as will permit him to savor humorous tidbits otherwise lost on us. Several times during the second act, to cite an instance, he was seen standing in his box with Mr. Moore beside him, smiling and applauding and Bravo-ing at the patter taking place, making us, as we have declared, all the more uncomfortable.

Poor benighted creature that we are, we find ourselves sorely tempted to enroll with Mr. Da Ponte at his academy over on Broadway Road, there to become acolytes in the Italian tongue, at least to such a degree that when someone on stage cracks a joke, we shall be able laugh at it . . . .

SIXTEEN

The Physician
How Da Ponte met his man

I can trace the beginning of his decline to the arrival of the great Pasta. Up to that time Lorenzo, already in his seventies, was as healthy as a horse. He had escaped the cholera with nothing more than a slight looseness of the bowels, probably occasioned by what I diagnosed as a mild effusion of the digestive system. I had always admired his constitution, the kind that we often observe in those rare individuals who look as if they are about to tumble into their graves but who somehow manage to cheat the devil and wind up outliving all their contemporaries, even to the next generation. There were those—now long since dead—who thought Da Ponte himself would have died eons ago; some, I dare say, even wished him dead, especially one in particular whom I have no desire to bring up. The fact is Lorenzo's energy was the equal of that of any two men, or women, for that matter. In those days just before Madame's arrival he seemed almost indefatigable. I don't know the details of all the arrangements he made, but they must have been demoralizing to a man of lesser confidence in his own abilities. Besides, there was something else driving him; all of us—his friends and acquaintances—saw it. As a medico, however, I will judge a man's condition by the signs of his body, not the sighs of his soul, so let all speculation on that score be laid to rest.

As for his constitution, as I've said, it was often belied by his frail appearance. It was that *appearance* of frailty that maybe kept him safe, who knows? Perhaps it was the seeming indifference to danger, which he showed through all his life that gave him a peculiar kind of immunity among the thugs, thieves and desperate men forever on the prowl.

One of those men, I remember, was Eli who served as Da Ponte's man for so many years. Lorenzo was often closed-mouthed about his alliance with this fellow. I think that the old man rather liked the aura of mystery about their partnership. It gave him pleasure to have the world presume that Eli appeared one day at his door in a kind of spontaneous incarnation. But the truth is—as I've heard Da Ponte tell it, with a chuckle—that his association with Eli began with a dispute over the size of an orange.

That dispute would certainly place the event at least twenty years ago, before Lorenzo had become one of us, when he was merely a traveling greengrocer and peddler of hard goods. Not that there is anything wrong with that, mind you. It would certainly put me in a bad light as a man if I failed to remember that I was not always a healer to the well-heeled; if I didn't recall in the glow of a kindly nostalgia those days when a visit to Tontine's was not to enjoy a bowl of chowder or a glass of spirits with friends, but to minister decoctions to carters or waiters, or to some livery man who got a fishbone caught in his throat.

But the tale of the orange that I started to tell you is one, as I've said, that Lorenzo took a special liking to. Perhaps he recognized in its outlines a kindred spirit in that street-smart man of his. Lorenzo told it one day, near the end, lying in his makeshift bed in the parlor of his academy. "I want to be near my books," he had said. He always had a sense of the melodramatic, especially in those final days.

The story brought a smile to his dry, crooked lips. He had been on his way back from a bad day, as he put it, and was about to put up his horse and wagon in the carriage house operated by the undertaker—"four cents a night they charged". Suddenly, this fellow comes shambling out between the buildings on Maiden Lane. He didn't look like a beggar exactly—and Lorenzo was quick to add that he was no Beau Brummel himself—but he had a species of gravity about him that one hungry man could always read in another.

Eli stood there with that look on his face, holding the traces of Lorenzo's horse.

"I'll have an orange, if you please, dad," was all he said.

It wasn't a demand, but the imperative nature of the claim was clear enough to Lorenzo, there in the wagon, who reached behind him and pulled out a sack. From it he withdrew a rolled-up bundle of cloth, and unwrapping that produced a soft, spongy sphere, neither orange nor yellow, but something, as Lorenzo admitted, that resembled the color of the film on one's teeth. First wiping it on his shirt, he offered it to Eli.

"Not a very healthy-looking orange," said Eli.

"Not a very healthy-looking customer," said Lorenzo.

The two looked at each other for a moment and Lorenzo continued:

"They're hard to get, and even harder to keep."

"I guess you can say that for men, too," said Eli.

"They're expensive," said Lorenzo.

"Oranges or men?" said Eli.

"Both", said Lorenzo. "I guess, then, you don't want the orange."

"I want it," said Eli, "But I don't expect to pay for it."

"I know I don't want a man," said Lorenzo. "This is a sole proprietorship."

"Well," said Eli. "It may be a sole proprietorship, but this is a pretty piss-poor orange."

"Take it or leave it," said Lorenzo.

"Well, then, I guess I'll leave it," said Eli. "For now, at any rate. Besides, I know where I can get better oranges and cheaper, too."

"Where?"

"Take me on and I'll tell you," said Eli.

"I cannot," said Lorenzo.

"Take it or leave it," said Eli.

And that's how they came together.

Lorenzo would never elaborate on how or where Eli found his oranges. You may say that the lapse of years and of his health caused Lorenzo to forget, but I think not. I've known him too long not to discern what I like to call a "mercantile jealousy" on his part.

That brand of caution is something I as a doctor can appreciate, when so many younger practitioners are coming up now who claim a greater cure for lesser maladies. There are a few, I'm told, who peremptorily disavow even bleeding, urging the lancet and the cupping glass to be put aside. I admit that bloodletting in the past has been too universally applied even in situations where cases of dropsy could be alleviated rather by purges than by leeches, but as a last resort, I consider bleeding to be an indispensable procedure. Da Ponte, himself, in fact, expressly requested to be bled during his last weeks. His protégé Mozart was bled, the old man declared, so was his Emperor. And was he, so impassioned by the literature and culture of the past, thus to be denied?

As for Eli's attitude toward their alliance, there was a rather florid aspect to it that over the years had become a ritual. Whenever Lorenzo assigned a task to him, Eli would take down from a hook his brown apron and, tying it around his waist, declare: "Labor calls."

Often the labor was simply the hauling of a crate of books from one room to another. Sometimes he was required to serve as butler. On more than one occasion—or so the story goes—Eli acted as Lorenzo's agent on the arrival of some ship with an unusual cargo. Doubtless there were other duties, as well, but whatever the assignment, trivial or momentous, Eli proceeded to his hook and to the donning of his apron, as if it were his uniform or a suit of armor.

But as I started to say, Da Ponte's decline began just after Pasta's triumph. I say "triumph" because the event was just as much a moral success for Lorenzo as it undoubtedly was a worldly one for Madame. She and her homunculus accepted the adulation almost as a matter of course. A few of us, like Clement Moore and me, detected a kind of iciness in her acceptance. Her smile, her outstretched arms as if in gracious gratitude, embraced a rather rehearsed quality hard to explain. She was not so much moved as inured. Her financial success, on the other hand, was a triumph of a different order. I've been told that she and her rabbit made a small fortune, perhaps even at Lorenzo's expense. Now that I think of it, it may have been this drain on his own resources that hastened his physical dissolution.

Certainly he had a haggard look that first night. I was crossing the lobby on my way upstairs to a box I shared with the Moore family when I saw Lorenzo sitting on a three-legged stool, perched uncomfortably behind a table. A pile of cheap, paper booklets lay on top. The stool was too low and he peered over the table's horizon like some helpless waif. The sight unaccountably touched me, for it was the only time he ever looked out of his element. What struck me was the way he seemed to slouch awkwardly, unfamiliarly, his elbows spraddling the table, his fingers barely touching the ragged edges of the booklets in front of him. He reminded me in some odd way of a beggar, some mendicant friar who had wandered into a strange, uncomfortable place. Yet, ironically, Lorenzo was precisely in circumstances that should have made him feel most at home.

As I approached him he smiled weakly and took one of the booklets from the top of the pile, offering it to me.

"No charge for you, my friend," he said. "Unless, of course, you'd care to make a contribution."

"A contribution to what, Lorenzo?"

"Why, to the Madame Pasta fund." He laughed sarcastically.

The booklet turned out to be the libretto. It was badly printed, but Lorenzo's name was clearly on the gray cover, both as author and translator. Who else, I thought, was in a better position to translate his own work?

"How did you find the time to do this?' I said. "You've been so busy?"

Lorenzo shrugged. "I don't eat," he said, and laughed again. He took up his libretto and opening to the first page, "Did you see the dedication?"

I opened my copy and read where he was pointing:

"In admiration for his genius,
to W.A. M."

"Who, exactly, is W.A.M.?" I asked, though I think now that I had guessed. Lorenzo only smiled.

The opera, of course, was a success, as was Madame Pasta, and, despite his precursive mood that night, Lorenzo must surely have enjoyed the excitement, the richness of the occasion, the cultural importance of the event.

But it was not long after that—after Pasta had gone back to Europe on a cold, rainy day—that Lorenzo seemed gradually to fail. At first he showed signs merely of fatigue. That was to be expected in a man of his age, taking into account the labor and stress of that Pasta period. I have always insisted on the danger of too much over-exertion, especially in regard to violent exercise, which tends rapidly to exhaust the nervous energy whereon the brain depends for its healthful activity. Not that Lorenzo ever seemed to credit my opinion on that matter. But soon his complexion took on a lean, ashy look; gone was the sureness, the aggressiveness of his gait. He moved as if with a limp, and when examining him one day I found an extensive induration of the popliteal space, followed shortly thereafter by periodic collapses.

When he lost his appetite I began to fear the worst. Ever since I had known him his appetite amounted almost to what I once jokingly called an iconoclasm of the stomach. The man could eat enormous amounts of food of every variety at any time of the day, in response to any occasion. Medically speaking, I regarded his digestive system as one of the seven wonders of the modern world, placing it perhaps just a shade below the Erie Canal or the new railroad. But when one day at Tontine's he turned away from his barely touched plate, I looked knowingly at Clement Moore who was sitting with us and he returned my look, as if to say, "And so it begins."

And, indeed, so it had. He was never the same again. As the days grew into weeks and the weather began to turn warmer, we knew that Lorenzo's time was near. We watched, without purposely watching, expected, without purposely expecting. When he finally took to bed we knew he would never get out of it.

*   *   *

SEVENTEEN

The Legatee
How Lorenzo Da Ponte paid his debts

It was almost as if Riley were expecting the news. He was not surprised when he saw me walk into the shop in a somber mood and I observed from his own quiet glance that he had sensed the reason for my visit. His greeting clearly showed that he had anticipated my announcement:

"Da Ponte's dead," he muttered, only half in declaration.

I need not have answered because when he looked down and saw the walking stick I was carrying he simply nodded.

"I see the old fellow's paid *his* debts," he added.

"Lorenzo always considered himself in my debt, you know," I said, almost in defense, though it seemed odd that I should defend myself by confirming the charge. "But if the truth be known, we were all pretty much in his."

Riley would certainly have understood the pertinence of such a remark. Over the years, the books he had obtained for and sold to Da Ponte, the legion of related works his students would have bought and paid for, must surely have helped put up the second story that now rose above us. There was even a reading room in the European manner, where on quiet, lonely days Da Ponte himself could be found among its shelves.

According to Riley, who spoke not in malice of a lost sale but in admiration of the old man's scholarly ways, Da Ponte often read several books in the course of a single afternoon. On cold, rainy days, when the heat from the new stove below settled itself among the stacks, making cozy even the most frigid of texts, you could sometimes hear the whisper of Da Ponte's voice as he mouthed the words, slowly, deliberately, curling the English language around the contours of his tongue as if in some private incantation.

I regret to say that my own works were not among these books. For all his informality, Riley was too much the gentleman to lie about their popularity and too much the businessman to take up shelf space with immovable objects. I know he keeps a pile of them somewhere out of sight in deference to my feelings.

"Yes," Riley said. "He's left behind more than his walking stick. Business is good."

"The country's growing up," I said. But it was a statement meant more to protect than explain. Riley was right. Lorenzo had bequeathed all of us a sense of culture which we would eventually have latched onto, but it was good to have gotten hold of it sooner than later. What I was trying to protect was a selfish sense of proprietorship that had nothing to do with opera or the number of books on Riley's second story reading room. What it came down to was a ruthless possessiveness that only grew stronger by the legacy of a gold-headed walking stick. The truth was that I did not want Riley or anyone else to claim a share in that special kinship that over the years had been aborning between Lorenzo and me. And though my head chided that no one could really share in anything so personal, my heart was jealous of such potential intimacy. I was like a child who had been given a rare gift. Though he knows it is forever his as he shows it to his friends, passing it around from hand to hand, he grows uneasy as he watches its progress around the group, anxious for its safe return into his own embrace.

It was thus with this childish anxiety that I refrained from telling Riley about the conversation I had with Da Ponte the day before he died. Dr. Francis was there, tending to him in the little sitting room where Da Ponte wished to be installed during his last illness, surrounded by his books and the odd assortment of mementos he had collected over the years. The worn out sofa which he had obtained through the auspices of Eli—none of us ever asked any questions about its provenance—had been augmented by chairs and ottomans, so that a reasonable facsimile of a bed had been fashioned. Lorenzo detested solitude; it only made him rusty, he declared, and the pleasant company of friends kept the hours moving and the mind healthily engaged. But all in all it was not a very comfortable arrangement. "I don't want to make myself too comfortable," he said to me when Dr. Francis had stepped out. "I'm not used to being comfortable. That's how I got to be as old as I am. My protégé, Mozart, was fond of saying that 'ease breed's dis-ease', and if anybody knew the bitter truth of that observation it was poor Wolfgang. No, my friend. I'm all right the way I am. Let's not shock my system into breaking down by departing from its lifetime of inconvenience."

The morning was rainy, and Lorenzo's sitting room—always chilly late in the year from the puny fires he habitually kept—"wood is dear", he used to say—was today actually stifling hot with half a forest's logs ablaze in the hearth. It occurred to me that the old man realized at last that the price of wood was of little import to him now. Then I recalled how insistent Dr. Francis was about warm rooms for sick patients. No doubt it was he, then, who had ordered the healthy fire.

Several times during our talk Eli had come in with more wood and dropped it on the hob. I noticed that he wasn't wearing his apron. He always made a point of displaying himself in it as if it was a uniform, and the pride he took in the act had become a standing joke between Francis and me.

Amid such heat I was surprised when Da Ponte asked me to add more wood to the already ravenous blaze. I reminded him that the hearth was already full and observed that one more piece of kindling would ignite a conflagration that would consume the entire city. He did not find my joke particularly funny. Instead, he simply glared at the hearth and said in a slow, deliberate tone: "Feed the fire. I want to keep the peddler out for a little while yet."

Here let me say that not once during his decline did Lorenzo give any sign of failing mental powers. But now, with his request to feed an already glutted fire and his remark about a peddler, I was beginning to think that the old man was starting to rave.

"I know he's coming for me," he declared.

And then, as if sensing my lack of faith, he looked me full in the face.

"Clement," he said. "I'm not mad. I'm sharing with you my final composition. If I had the time or the strength, or even the will, I would put it into verse. But I'm not going to buy his wares. Not yet. Not today. He'll be here soon enough. Feed the fire."

I was sitting quietly when Eli came into the room.

"There's some fellow outside. Said he was passing by and meant to pay a visit to an old shipmate."

"Shipmate?" I asked.

"He said it kinda slyly, like it was a private joke. I asked his name but he snorted, and then held out this here book. 'Give this to Da Ponte,' he says. 'He'll know me.'"

I took the book, an old dog-eared collection of sermons, and gave it to Da Ponte. I saw his eyes gleam and a smile enliven his face.

"Why, it's Humpfnagel!" he said.

"Hello, you old spell-binder," the fellow barked, Eli having let him in and closing the door on his way out. "I've always told myself I'd look you up."

"I'm glad to see you," Da Ponte said, hoisting himself higher in the bed. "Have you read the book?"

"I'm not much for sermons . . ." The fellow looked at me and saw plainly the circumstances into which he had tumbled.

"It's good of you to come all this way to give it back. I only lent it to you, you know."

"Yes," said the fellow.

"Mr. Moore, this is the man who started me off on my career. He was, in effect, my first investor. Now then, sir, I believe I owe you ten dollars, am I right."

The man cast me a glance.

"You've got a good memory. Ten dollars exactly, it was, not counting any interest. But I guess I can collect it some other time," he said.

"Nonsense," said Da Ponte. "I always pay my debts. See my man on the way out. Tell him I said to take care of you."

The fellow stood there uncomfortably. He looked at me and shrugged.

"Well," he said. "I've got to be going. Rest easy."

Da Ponte waved his hand in farewell, but the fellow had already gone.

In the course of my life I have seen men in their last moments recant the shameful events of their lives; some had found peace and talked genially, as if at dinner over a bottle of wine. A few had no regrets and contented themselves with the quiet comfort of a hand within their own. Most were too weak, too incoherent, too physically depleted to care much for anything. But Da Ponte seemed to act as if he were on perpetual display, like the Catholics with their Monstrance during Holy Week. To me he always appeared to be performing a scene from an opera, without the words or the music, but always with the gesture. When he called to Eli for his walking stick, I would not have been surprised to see him arise from his couch, raising the stick heavenwards, staggering as if to the front of the stage, and then collapsing as the curtain closed. Lorenzo would have admired his own melodramatic death as a fitting testament to a life so fiercely lived. I say that I would not have been surprised, but the oddity is that for all its melodrama I would have inexplicably approved of the thing, in spite of its rather lurid appeal. That was the effect Lorenzo had on me: forcing me to have faith in the truth of contradiction, to believe in the virtue of perversity.

When Eli brought him his stick, Lorenzo waited for him to leave before addressing me.

"I want you to have this", he said. "I needn't tell you why. You have been my American emperor. Who else should I give it to? Take it. Mozart wouldn't mind."

"I'd like to think he would approve," I said, risking the appearance of vanity in order to conceal my embarrassment. But reading me well, as he almost always did, Lorenzo smiled. "I'm glad you said it," he declared. "Now feed the fire."

We spent the next few minutes talking of minor things that in other times would have been important. I asked him if he planned next year to arrange another opera season. He simply smiled and I could tell he knew I was clumsily trying to spare him the fear of death by pretending in a future. It was a traitorous act on my part. As a clergyman I should have had the courage of my convictions and preached to him of eternity and the saving of his soul. But as I have been trying to say—and thereby aid my own understanding of it all—Da Ponte struck me as possessing a different kind of soul. He was not so much incredulous to the possibility of salvation as he was competitively alert to its opportunities. Perhaps another Mozart was waiting to be discovered, another protégé, another America? Who knows?

Soon Dr. Francis returned and Lorenzo and I shook hands, knowing it was the last time we would see one another together this side of paradise. Of course, Lorenzo would be there, virtuous charlatan that he was.

The next day I was told that Dr. Francis had arrived early in the morning, and when he entered the sitting room knew by the chill that the fire was out. He knew also, as he approached the bed that during the night the peddler had indeed come.

*   *   *

Edwards Brothers, Inc.
Thorofare, NJ USA
November 21, 2011